A E

Steve Frazee

GUNSMOKE

WESTERNS

First published 1960
by The Hearst Corporation

This hardback edition 1994
by Chivers Press
by arrangement with
the Golden West Literary Agency
in association with Laurence Pollinger Ltd.

ISBN 0 7451 4589 2

British Library Cataloguing in Publication Data available

Printed and bound in Great Britain by
Redwood Books, Trowbridge, Wiltshire

THE WAR of the Second Confederacy actually did not begin in earnest until after Denver, hastily fortified by Colonel Edward R. Trevarthen, remained the only white man's outpost between Eastern Kansas and the Great Salt Lake—excepting, of course, the Army camp nearby.

Those early military debacles following the Indians' singularly united defiance of the Order of 1868 were but preliminary skirmishes which many construed merely as stunning proof of the Army's sad decline since the spring of three years before.

Settlers, ranchers, traders, miners—all the others who had saved their lives by abandoning most of a million square miles of mountains and plains—had no criticism of the Army, except to howl that there wasn't nearly enough of it. But when the first major campaign began, on July 1, 1869, the only ones who complained about the size of the Army were those who had to eat its dust.

Even then, few among those marching or riding toward battle appreciated the enormity of their job. But at least one who watched their coming knew what they faced.

In the Moon of Cherries Reddening that white men call July, Iron Buffalo stood near his pony on a hill among the trembling trees, looking with far-seeing glasses at blue columns coming slowly toward him.

Twenty thousand—as the white men count—they were, led by a little soldier chief who had been powerful in the white men's war among themselves. Winding down the rolling hills they came, riders moving slowly, wagons side by side in fours—all the wagons from the white man's world, it seemed. Long lines of walking soldiers came behind the foremost riders. Behind the walking soldiers, far ahead and to the sides were more blue riders.

No Indian ever had looked upon an army as large as this.

Dust smoke blotted out the sunshine, rising toward the Shining Mountains where the moccasin of winter still was heavy.

No Indian scouts rode for pay money wide beyond this army. The horsemen scouting trouble far ahead and on the sides were old mountain men with hairy faces, men who knew the paths among these far-rising rocks almost as well as the Black Indians who owned this land.

In the big winter camp, where mountains met the wide, free buffalo lands, the little soldier chief had left twenty circles of blue-coats, many of them sick. So said Sunfish, the young white man now with the Brules and Unkpatilas who were watching the little army coming up the Arkansas.

Iron Buffalo took the far-seeing eyes from his face and looked at the high, cold places where camped old warriors with sun-trapping mirrors, taken when the broad Comanches captured the last big wagon train. The old warriors could make the spirit of the sun leap from one high place to another, twinkling down the mountains, telling Indians many far miles away just what the army was doing. So it had been when scouting parties came. Those who had tried to find the Indians in the broad parks and green thickets had not been harmed.

But all were dead of the six scouting parties that had tried to ride across the mountains toward the Indians' big camp in the long valley where the grass was good.

Though the Shining Mountains stood all around up here, like giant buffalo with winter's breath upon their backs, the rolling lands between were wide, broad and big for war.

Blue men and dust came closer. Down the years that Iron Buffalo could remember, even before his first breechclout, blue men had been making dust ever closer to the setting sun. Now the time was here to stop them. The warriors were here, and, for the first time in the memory of Indians, the guns were here.

Still Iron Buffalo was not happy. Let the young men look with black hate at the dust smoke. Let *them* dance and boast and laugh, planning greatness for the fighting.

War on the white man was not good, but tomorrow might be the time for it, a day to count time from.

Iron Buffalo went toward his pony, limping from the hurt of a knee wounded four winters ago in the fighting at Julesburg. He was not tall, less by the width of a big man's palm than had been his Cheyenne father. His dark-brown hair hung loose above his faded blanket. His hands were long and slender. From the back he might have been a warrior who had counted no coups, taken no scalps.

Tall and grave beside his spotted pony, Fighting Bear, father of Iron Buffalo's Brule wife, moved his old eyes from the dust and spoke.

"They are many."

Iron Buffalo would have stepped upon a rock to mount his pony easily, but, concealing what was known, he leaped upon the horse, his thin face not showing how the pain knives stabbed and twisted in his knees.

In the eyes, and in the lean, long lips, Fighting Bear saw the power that made Iron Buffalo not only a strong warrior but a man whose words in council made the heart believe, even when there had been much doubt before listening. Half Oglala, half Cheyenne, Iron Buffalo was a strange man who did not smile often, but when he walked through camp in his poor robes little children ran to him without fear, full of shouts and questions.

If Iron Buffalo had little fat ones rolling in his lodge he might smile more, Fighting Bear thought, deciding to go once more to the old women and the Holy Men. Yet far behind his face old Fighting Bear knew that it was not his daughter's fault there were no children in the lodge. These things sometimes were, even when the man was a strong warrior and a good husband.

"We are many," Iron Buffalo said.

It was so, Fighting Bear thought. There were thousands from the seven councils of the Tetons that were but one of seven councils of all the Dakotas: the tall Cheyennes, who, like the Sioux, had lost many helpless ones before the white man's treachery; Snakes and Crows, ancient enemies of the Tetons, had taken the pipe for this great war; there were thousands from the northern plains and forests—Blackfeet, Assiniboin, Shoshoni, Nez Percé, Flatheads, Spokan, Pend Oreille, Palouse, Cree and Chippewa; warriors from the southern plains—Shawnees, Comanches, Kiowa, Arickaree, Arapaho, little brown Apaches far from their dry lands; the Black Indians of the mountains and their brothers, the Piutes; and many others, some from tribes whose language was strange even in the sign talk.

"When these are gone—" looking at the dust smoke, Fighting Bear moved both closed hands in front and to the left, then opened them three times, palms down—"many more will come in anger. As the grasshoppers they will come."

"It is so." Iron Buffalo looked gravely at his wife's father. "Would you have us stay scattered and weak on the plains? Here we can fight. Then we can go back to our homes until we have to join and fight again." The slender chief watched the army. "We will never keep our homes unless we fight, and our children will have to fight when we are gone."

"I know these things. I saw these things before your father wore a breechclout," old Fighting Bear said, rebuking him. "The white heart is bad, the tongue is forked. Peace will be their peace, not ours. You have grown strong by wanting nothing but to save our people, even people who were our enemies, but . . ." Old Fighting Bear looked with troubled eyes upon the dust clouds.

"It will be a bad thing," Iron Buffalo agreed. "Not like the little battles of last summer when we killed two hundred at the River Crossing, three hundred on the Smoky Trail—the other little fights. But would you have us lose our country, be put in places like the Otoes and the Kaws we saw on our way to the Great White Chief's lodge in the place called Washington?"

Fighting Bear still watched the Army. "That is not good, but . . ."

Anger pounded drums in Iron Buffalo's head, but he wore the face that had turned strong words and dissension in many councils, as a smooth rock parts muddy waters growling past it. "Where are the ones who went to talk beside the white flag, with the soldiers after the fighting on Bow River?"

Fighting Bear did not answer. For an instant the warrior lights burned in his eyes. But it was mostly with sadness that he looked upon the army bending like blue water across the plain.

"After tomorrow there can be no peace." Fighting Bear was heavy in mounting his pony. "But still I will wish for some other way."

Where dust was thick enough to choke a statue, stocky Billy Munro stumbled along with the infantry, no longer shrugging irritably at the weight of blue wool and sweat upon his shoulders. When he'd mustered with Company J at dawn three days ago at Camp Pike, his long breech-loading Springfield had been the gleaming weapon of a soldier going forth to glory. Now it was a thing to carry, a heavy, dusty burden that poured sweat and finger aches from its steel butt plate. Tonight he wouldn't care if he cleaned and oiled it or not—but he knew that Sergeant Mullins would.

Even in his tiredness, Munro looked around him with the grasping curiosity of healthy youth in his clear brown eyes. His eighteen years rode lightly on his sweating, dust-streaked face. He really wasn't half as weary as he thought, having reserves of strength that he hadn't learned of yet.

But Munro was greatly dissatisfied with war, if you could call it that. You lay in camp all winter, drilling, drilling, doing work that had to be done again in a few hours. Then suddenly you're kicked out and marched sixty miles in three days, with all the horses in the army throwing dust in your face. Maybe it had been different in the Civil War. If he hadn't been so young, he could have got in that. Maybe in the cavalry. They got the best of everything. And didn't they know it, too! But if he'd been in just the infantry in the war, maybe he'd be used to walking, like wiry, grinning Dan Beavers, who slouched along all day, hardly taking a drink of water, and then visited all over the camp at night.

Munro looked sidewise and up at the pug-nosed, red-stubbled face under the dusty forage cap. Brown grime and the smell of sweat were just as heavy on Beavers as anyone else. There was nothing about him to show that he'd fought Indians on the plains and then Rebels for four years—unless it was that Beavers never seemed bothered about anything. Maybe that was it. Beavers sure didn't care much about things, or else he wouldn't have been busted from a sergeant so many times.

Taller by a head than Munro, Beavers saw the look and grinned. "The first thousand miles, Billy Boy, and then you're in! What was it they told you—sign for a couple of years, but of course the Indians would be scared to death and peaceful in a few months, and then you could get your bonus and go home?"

"They didn't fool me any," Munro said. Private William A. Munro, Company J First Regiment, Special Indian Volunteers, Department of Missouri. He looked at the grim wedges of the mountains and thought that Missouri sure covered a lot of territory, the way the Army put it. And what was so blamed "special" about being walked to death in dust that would gag a dog?

Lean, black-bearded Burt Johannes laughed. "They didn't fool Billy none!"

Laughter coursed lightly along the company.

Beavers rolled dust in his throat and spat in a trampled spot from which the man ahead had just removed his heel. He grinned at Munro. "Like I always say, Billy, everybody in the Army is a liar but me and Old Stub—and sometimes you can't even trust the general."

"You ought to know, Beavers," Johannes said, grinning. "You're around his headquarters so much some of these green ones think you're an aide."

"We got to know what's going on," Beavers said.

"What *is* going on, Danny?" someone several rows behind called.

Wrinkled, brown-faced Sergeant Mullins, both hair-fringed ears on the conversation, one eye warily on his immediate superior riding a tall sorrel horse where the dust was not quite so thick, turned his head and shouted: "Shut up and march, you squareheads!"

The talking continued in subdued tones, making it necessary for Sergeant Mullins to listen carefully, one eye still cocked on the lieutenant on the sorrel.

"Well," Beavers said, "Old Stub is worried about no couriers from Freeland's army. Then he keeps muttering about the light cannon and Gatlings the Indians took off them supply trains last summer. And he's still sore about them six scouting parties that started over the mountains and never came back."

"It's that danged Iron Buffalo!" Johannes said. "He's got all the Indians stirred up with that Holy War talk of his."

The name ran up and down the column.

"He's half Comanche and half Sans Arc."

"Aw hell! He's all Sioux."

"Cheyenne."

"What's the difference? They're all savages of some kind. Iron Buffalo is a great big tough son—"

"Naw! He's sort of spindly and plain-looking, with a club foot—"

"Club foot, your eye! He got shot in the leg at River Crossing—or some place."

"Well, if he can make the Indians stick together, he's

the one old Abe ought to've sent down to talk to Jeff Davis a few years ago."

"*Show* me any Indians that stick together!"

"Hell, I can't even show you any that don't. We look for 'em on the plains. They ain't there. Now we look in the mountains. They likely ain't here, neither."

"Those six scouting parties must have found 'em."

"I betcha Indian scouts could've found 'em and got back."

"Where's your Indian scouts—since the Pawnees got cold feet? Then even the Kaws they bribed off the reservation got scared out here and sneaked home."

Sergeant Mullins gauged the lieutenant's steam pressure accurately. "Shut up and march!" the sergeant yelled. This time he meant it.

Wagon wheels broke turf, skirling dust from iron tires. Infantrymen splashed along in the fine dirt, now and then stumbling a little over small rocks. On the flanks, a mile behind, and far ahead cavalry rode easily, cursing the necessity of keeping pace with infantry. So far out they were dark specks on the immense piece of prairie trapped by mountains, old mountain men rode in pairs, keen-eyed, reading all the signs there were to read.

For weeks the country had been scouted, and pony tracks had been few. Now they were even more scarce.

Billy Munro felt his sun-blistered nose and rolled his shoulders under the hot clamp of sweat. "You know for sure where Old Stub is taking us?"

"Somewhere up here where the mountains run together. About day after tomorrow we meet Freeland. Then I guess we camp while scouting parties ride here and there. When we're short of grub and the Indians have run off some mules and horses, we go back to Camp

Pike and get ready to spend another winter drilling and scratching."

Munro tried to sound casual. "Won't the Indians fight?"

Beavers laughed. "This army? They'll chop up scouting parties and let us run in circles, but they're not going to tangle with sixteen, seventeen thousand men." The red-stubbled face was serious for a moment. "I'd hate to think what they might do if they really did learn to use them guns they swiped." He grinned. "Fine joke on us, huh, Billy? Us with no artillery."

"That's not so blame funny," Munro said so seriously that those who heard him laughed.

A courier with a yellow neckerchief whipping his chin galloped unnecessarily close to the plodding column, and sullen curses followed him. Stringing dust and broken wisps of dry grass flew from the shallow cups of the horse's shoes as it caught up with Company J.

Dan Beavers cursed the courier violently. Sergeant Mullins twisted his wrinkled face and spewed tobacco juice against the rider's leg. The courier waved at the cursing men and laughed.

A few moments later the lieutenant on the sorrel horse broke through the dust. "Let's have a little military order here, Sergeant!"

"Yes, sir!" Mullins said. He turned to bellow at the company.

An obscene mutter followed the lieutenant as he rode away from the thick dust, wiping grit from his teeth against the fringes of his gauntlet.

Hot and dusty, slow as the slowest man, wagons dipping earth, the army went deeper into the mountains toward the rendezvous with Freeland's powerful scouting force, which was now coming up the Arkansas on a parallel course forty miles south as the crow flies.

No member of Old Stub's command, not even the bearded mountain men, had seen an Indian since leaving Camp Pike.

Moonlight lay cold on gray rocks along the pass where countless hoofs of ponies, recently stripped for war, had preceded Simon Bullard, army deserter, seven years a white brother to the Crows. His tremendous weight sat brutally on an undersized pony. Black weasel-wrapped braids hung beside a curling black beard. Smeared with stain from many cooking fires, the thick, loose skin of his forehead crawled with every movement of his wide-set, bulging eyes.

Ebony marbles in white rings, his eyes rolled alertly toward every sound of the night.

Grievances, sullen anger, unsettled bitterness—obscure thoughts of many kinds threshed in twisting disorder in his mind. He tried to weigh one hate, one thought, against another.

Out of all the murky turmoil he didn't know for sure why he kept on riding to warn the soldiers about those guns. He didn't know for sure that he *would* keep on riding. But he did.

Mainly it was the jeering of the squaws.

A fine thing! Iron Buffalo didn't trust him, not even after the weeks he'd spent in showing the damned Indians how to load and fire the light cannons and Gatling guns. That hadn't been so easy, what with the fools yelping like scared dogs at first and running away every time they fired a round; the Flatheads that went loony and crawled under the limber with their arms over their heads; the crazy Apache chief who seared his shoulder on the hot Gatling barrels and then wanted to kill Bullard. But he'd stayed with it, taking that smooth talk from Iron Buffalo, until the stinking Indians knew how to load and fire the guns as well as anybody, even if only a few of them ever did catch on to the idea about aiming instead of just shooting to hear a big noise.

Still, some of the Nez Percé had got pretty smart about elevation and ranges.

After all that hard work, that lousy cold-faced Iron Buffalo had ordered him, Simon Bullard, to stay behind with the old men and squaws and kids in the big camp over the mountains.

In spite of the squaws' dirty remarks, there were a good many unclear answers in Simon Bullard's head. He couldn't stay with the army very long. Somebody would be sure to remember about that officer he'd killed, and then the provost guard he'd strangled while escaping after the court-martial. Nothing in his life had made Simon Bullard, one-time artillery sergeant, as scared as sitting in the guardhouse, waiting, just waiting there for a detail to come and put a rope around his neck.

It might be better to stick with the Indians. Iron Buffalo would give him the ponies promised for teaching the Indians how to handle the guns. He could go back North with his Crow wives and take things easy again. It would be pretty good to be one of the all-fired few who could live in Indian country and keep his hair. The Indians were all right. They wouldn't want to hang him for killing someone that needed killing. They didn't call him Cannibal either, just because he'd been forced to eat parts of his first Crow wife and her brother that time snow trapped the three of them in the Yellowstone country. They would have died of starvation anyway.

Cannibal Bullard. What a devil of a name. Every white man he ran across knew him by that. What if the Indians wouldn't go trapping alone with him any more; still, they didn't call him Cannibal.

Bullard stopped the pony. His protruding eyes rolled at funeral-gray rocks as he sat there in cold moonlight. He hadn't made a decision so far. He'd merely acted. Now he tried to think about it.

In the end the jeering of the squaws won.

Cannibal Bullard rode on up the pass.

His big, wild laugh rang out among the cold stones.

Near the headwater of Badger Creek, twenty miles south of Old Stub's bivouacked army, Rafe Winburn rested in the rocks a few minutes while he inspected the piece of horsehide around his wounded leg. Moonglow was bright on his long gray hair and short beard. It lifted gloom from the hollows of his eyes, but behind his eyes were other shadows that would not lift so easily, a darkness caused by what he'd seen and heard in Ute Canyon that afternoon.

Back there in the smoke, among the rocks and cedars and piñons, lay the wreckage of fifteen hundred men. He was, as far as he knew, the only survivor.

After a while he rose slowly, first lifting the muzzle of his Henry rifle so that it would not tap a rock and ring out in the waiting night. After a few steps the pain in his leg started again. Soon he'd have to break out of the rocks entirely and strike across open park land if he wanted to reach Old Stub's army somewhere on the South Platte before dawn. If he didn't make it before light, he most likely wouldn't ever make it.

Well, he'd been up against worse during his thirty-five years in these mountains. Tonight he felt the drag of those years as though they were a century.

He left the rocks and went boldly into the cold light of the open grasslands.

Splitting forces on a deal like this morning was simple-minded. He'd told Freeland so, right to his clean-shaved, narrow face, when the general first got excited about wanting to chase the two or three hundred Cheyennes that had gone hauling up Ute Canyon trail like they were scared to death. At first Wilburn couldn't believe Freeland was serious, but the general really was.

"It's a raw stall if I ever saw one!" Winburn protested. "The gulch is wide for five, six miles and then there's a tight canyon—just the kind of place they love to suck a few companies into."

Freeland looked down his thin nose and stuck out his big chin. "I appreciate your interest, Winburn, but I'm accustomed to getting military advice from my staff, not civilian scouts."

"But, General, let me tell you—"

Freeland raised one hand. Winburn could see it yet, long fingers in a trim chrome gauntlet, with black marks of bridle reins and sweat across the palm. "That is quite enough, Winburn!"

So one half of Freeland's cavalry, led by Brigadier Masterson, got ready to chase after Indians who had gone up a gulch. Accurately but reluctantly, Winburn and the other scouts admitted that the gulch led to South Park just as readily as the pass thirty miles up the valley.

"But not nearly so safe," Winburn protested. "It's a bad deal, Freeland."

The general scowled, regretting the fact that scouts were outside the strictness of military discipline. He made a sharp, bitter comment on that fact. Some of the officers about him laughed, though Colonel Trevarthen was stone-faced and silent. "Our nervous friend speaks of safety," Freeland said, smiling. "Gentlemen, there is no safety in war, I've found; but after all we're not looking for safety. We're looking for Indians, and I fear the little handful that scampered away is probably the largest collection we'll see in all these mountains. I would like very much to wipe them out." His big jaw snapped shut. "Gentlemen, follow your orders!"

Fifteen hundred cavalry, one thousand infantry, the horse herd and all the mule packs of ammunition went up the valley with General Freeland.

Masterson took his command up a little stream that wound among bronze-colored cedar and piñon-spotted hills.

Flanking parties rode the tops of the gulch; high above them scouts fought rocks and tangled patches of trees. One company trailed a quarter of a mile behind the main body in the gulch. Couriers from the advance detail reported at half-hour intervals. Finally they reported that the tracks of the fleeing Cheyennes had spread into a hundred or more individual trails on both sides of the gulch.

The passage began to steepen into a canyon. To keep pace with the main body, those companies riding the flanks had to drop lower and lower. High above them Winburn was leading his horse most of the time. Just before the gulch became a canyon, the scout looked down and saw piled across the trail a solid mass of cedar and piñon trees laid three or four feet deep and two hundred feet long in the gulch bottom.

The column halted. Masterson and two officers rode forward with the messenger from the advance detail.

Winburn went on. For a while he had seen pony tracks occasionally. Now he was finding none. Looking back, he saw cavalry scouting up the slopes around the pile of trees. Slow as it would be, he thought, the thing to do would be to lead the column around the canyon rim, though it would mean three or more hours of lost time. Even so, they weren't going to catch those Cheyennes anyway. Well, he wasn't running things, as Freeland had mentioned. He looked at rugged masses of canyon-scarred hills rising in series after series on both sides of the canyon, and went on.

Later, when red cliffs had forced him back downhill almost to the canyon edge, he saw another tree block near the head of the canyon. It was almost as high as the head of the advance rider sitting his horse before it.

Winburn looked back. The last of the column, riding two abreast, was passing the first pile of trees. He had a sudden feeling of deadly uneasiness. "I don't like it!" he muttered to his horse.

He felt a little better when he saw the rear detail stop and dismount near the first tree block. Troopers began to seek the shade of rocks. Fair enough, Winburn thought. Masterson was not taking the chance of having the trees burned before he got clear of the canyon.

Winburn mounted and started to ride on, studying the broken rocks on his right.

He felt the blow against his leg and heard the shot. The next instant his horse was squealing as it went, in running bucks, straight for a dense tangle of cedar. Limbs tore at Winburn's beard, whipped his eyes into smarting blindness. He held to his rifle and left the horse. Dead limbs splintered as they ripped across his buckskin jacket. He bounced on the thick needle mat and rolled till a tree stopped him. He heard his horse crashing on ahead, still screaming in mortal agony.

Rifle fire broke out in scattered blasts. Shouts, cries, a few loud whoops, the sounds of running feet came to him from both sides of the trees. For a few moments the crash of rifle fire was irregular. Then it came like the bursting of threads in ripping canvas.

On hands and knees, shaking moisture from his eyes, Winburn crawled as far up the hill as the cedars gave concealment. Firing was steady now, unpunctuated by howls and yells. He blinked until he could see clearly, then inched to the edge of the cedars and peered through the branches.

Less than a hundred feet away, seven Indians were lying behind rocks, taking their time about shooting down into the canyon. Winburn stared hard, startled for the moment out of all concern for his own position.

Bannocks! Hundreds of miles south of their own country. The vague stories of a great Holy War union of Indians must be true.

A boy of thirteen or fourteen, a brand-new army knapsack slung on one bare shoulder, walked up behind the riflemen and said something. A lean-jawed, pox-pitted warrior twisted around and spoke angrily. The boy squatted hastily, his knapsack striking solidly against the rocks. In one hand he held a box of cartridges. All seven of the Indians were shooting what looked like new Springfield rifles. Two of them had army revolvers stuck in the thongs of their breechclouts.

This wasn't Indian fighting, Winburn thought. It was organized war, based on the Indians' favorite tactics.

Across the canyon the rocks seemed to move as masses of warriors rushed to the top of the passage. They took cover quickly. More came from behind them. When

Winburn looked again at his own side a dozen or more Gros Ventres were crowding for shooting room beside the Bannocks. More were coming up. All were armed with rifles. Another young ammunition carrier had joined them.

Down in the canyon the cavalry had dismounted. Horses were plunging and rearing. Thirty or forty fear-crazed or wounded animals had broken loose and were smashing around in the tightly packed column. Non-coms and officers were shooting the worst of them when they could.

Puffs of gunfire began to increase from the canyon. Bullets whipped through the cedars above Winburn. A kneeling Gros Ventre slid forward on his face, sprawling over his rifle. One of the ammunition carriers reached for the weapon. The lean-jawed Bannock shoved him away and pointed to the knapsack.

Winburn saw officers getting the rear of the column started down the canyon toward the first brush block, where the sides were easy to climb. He saw Colonel Trevarthen high in the stirrups on his big black horse. Trevarthen and others were signaling the threshing, wounded column. Soon the jam began to loosen.

The Indians anticipated the movement. They concentrated fire on the lower end of the blue mass. Horses began to pile up. For a moment they threatened to block the way. Then Trevarthen's gleaming black leaped the struggling tangle, and troopers began to follow.

Even as hoofs were in the air above the pile of wounded and dead animals, Winburn saw a man work free and try to crawl away. Three troopers tried to clear the jumble side by side. An iron gray, the edges of its saddle blanket clean yellow through the smoke, was jostled in mid-leap, and its forelegs hit the pile of flesh. The horse drove hard to hold its feet. One rear foot struck the crawling man and rolled him on his side. The horse threshed wildly. It cleared the pile in a humping lurch and carried its rider down the canyon.

The crawling trooper began to move again, more slowly. Lead from the canyon rim found him. He lay still, one of the many blue figures lying motionless.

Officers began to break loose dismounted men plastered against the rocks. Some fired as they ran. Some clung to stirrups. Those waiting for the packed mass to unloosen laid down a heavy fire against the canyon edges.

Winburn felt a lift of spirit at the cold courage of those blue men fighting back from a murderous situation.

The covering fire for the withdrawal settled to well-directed, deadly shooting. All the Indians near Winburn were flat now. Lead was buzzing from the rocks, dropping lower into the cedars. Winburn pressed hard against the needle mat. The scout's stomach twisted coldly when he saw fresh wave after wave of warriors come to the canyon edge and then lie down. Others higher on the hill were leaping in the direction of the retreat.

And yet there had been little whooping. The loudest sound besides gunfire was the screaming of horses from the canyon.

Winburn wondered about his own mount. He hoped the Indian who had wounded him thought he had been carried on down the hill with the horse. When the struggle lessened the Indian was sure to come looking through the cedars. That would have to be faced when it happened.

He saw the first riders reach the slopes above the

lower pile of trees and try to gallop up the sides, but their horses were too large against the fire. Survivors leaped to the ground, and rolling animals crushed some of them. Dismounted now, Trevarthen stayed below, directing coolly. As riders reached him they dismounted and drove their horses on down the gulch. By twos and threes the cavalry began to surge up both slopes, straight into the terrible fire.

At first, half of the blue men were falling. More and more came pounding down the sandy bottom. More riderless horses galloped toward the brush block. The rear detail clubbed them on down the gulch to make room for more. Blue clumps grew and spread on the slopes, going upward in short charges, building power behind them, firing from cover to protect those rushing ahead.

A few Indians near the mouth of the canyon began to rise to fire. More than a few of them began to fall.

We're going to make it! Winburn exulted. Once on the rims the troopers could sweep along them, diverting fire from those yet to follow. Winburn calmly selected the first Indian he was going to kill, the lean-jawed, pox-pitted Bannock.

Then the scout saw fire arrows arching toward the lower pile of piñon and cedar. The company at the barrier was putting up a blazing fight against the Indians creeping ever lower. A fire started. A trooper ran from behind a rock and fought it with his hands. More arrows fell, and little blazes began to grow. The cavalrymen used blankets. Some stripped their tunics and beat against the flames. They began to lie still on the block of boughs, blue uniforms against the dull-green trees. Smoke lifted around one trooper lying face down. Two ran to drag him back, and one of them fell beside the wounded man. The other staggered back to cover, doubled over.

More fire arrows arched from the canyon rim. The trees began to burn.

Wood smoke mingled with the acrid fumes of burned gunpowder. The breeze that had been gentle in the shaded canyon ten minutes before became a crackling wind. Smoke and embers began to sweep between the walls, as up a chimney.

Then the Indians began to whoop.

Cut off by smoke, gasping in the hot blast, some of those not yet untangled from the snarl began to scale the steep sides. Some lost their carbines as they clutched for holds. The Indians picked them off. Small groups fought up together and reached the rim, but Winburn saw none who got farther.

Riderless horses snorted, piercing sounds of terror. They ran wild, trampling dismounted men, crushing some of those who were running and trying to get down the canyon where the strongest climbing attempt was underway.

Flames spread to trees clinging to the canyon sides.

Through the haze of heat and smoke Winburn saw Masterson lead the head of the column up the passage. A little later the upper pile of trees began to blaze. Horses whirled, crushed struggling, frantic men against the rocks, then bolted down the canyon to trample or disorganize those still trying to get up.

The upper blaze was a solid barrier.

Soldiers yelled. Horses going mad with terror emitted chilling screams. Louder than gunfire or the shrieks of Indians came the crackling, roaring, bursting sound of flames.

All co-ordination was lost.

The Indians whooped and fired.

Troopers scrambled to get out the best way they could, some working along the walls to join Trevarthen's men. Survivors of the rear detail already had joined Trevarthen. Now and then Winburn saw the colonel, mounted once more, high in the stirrups, still directing the fight.

When the attack toward the rim on Winburn's side began to falter, Trevarthen rode the big black up through the rocks. Men followed him, and many of them reached the top. Winburn heard heavy shooting for a long time. Then the blasts of rifle and carbine fire began to dwindle, and not long after that the only shooting came from the Indians.

Coming straight out of the decreasing smoke, directly at the Bannocks and Gros Ventres ahead of Winburn, a dark-haired cavalryman labored through the rocks. His forage cap was gone, and so was his carbine, but he held a pistol in his left hand. Strands of hair were sweat-plastered over one side of his forehead. His mouth was open with his heavy breathing, and his eyes were wild and scared. He paused a moment, gasping for air, holding the pistol before him defensively.

The lean-jawed Bannock who had reminded the ammunition carrier of his duty twisted and handed his rifle to the same lad, crouched behind him. The boy's knapsack was light now, Winburn saw.

The trooper coughed and started up the hill. His boots slipped, and he put one hand down to hold himself. When he straightened the Indian boy shot him in the chest.

Winburn raised his Henry from the needle mat, then slowly let it down.

From under the Gros Ventre who had died in the first

of the fighting the Bannock jerked the dead man's rifle. He tossed it to the boy.

Smoke still drifted over the canyon, but the sounds of flames and firing were dying. When moving blue showed through a rift Indian muzzles trained and spat. And then the firing fell until it no longer hid the sounds of wounded on the slopes and in the canyon.

Rafe Winburn was sixty years old. For thirty-five years he had lived in the mountains and on the western edges of the plains where death and violence had not been strangers to him. He put his cheek against the needles, swallowed a vile taste and barely kept from vomiting.

Scattered shooting was still sounding when bone whistles shrilled across the canyon. The Indians in front of Winburn yelled and began to run down the slopes. He turned his head and saw that the other side of the canyon was erupting with leaping, screaming figures.

The cries of the wounded began to stop.

Winburn, moving cautiously, reached back to feel his wounded calf. It had been bleeding slowly. He waited for a few moments, until the ground in front of him was clear. Then he started to leave the cedars.

Close down the hill from where he lay he heard the light sound of moccasins. As his rifle twisted around it snapped a tiny dead twig from a limb. He reached with his left hand and jerked the limb aside. Ten feet away an Oglala warrior was staring at him, a yellow paint spot on each cheekbone. Just the Indian's head showed above a screen of cedars.

Winburn fired the rifle with one hand. He heard the sodden chop of the bullet striking flesh and bone. The warrior fell. In a moment all but the smallest of the stiff-limbed branches were quiet.

The scout waited, listening to a few shots in the trees

farther down the canyon edge. Then he left the cedars, working from rock to rock, from one small clump of trees to another. Two hundred yards away he cut a strip of hide from Trevarthen's dead horse, wondering vaguely how the animal had come so far with its entrails hanging out and one front shoulder almost shot away. He crawled into a stand of twisted red cedars and bound the bloody hide tight around his wound.

Two Bannock chiefs came up from the canyon rim and walked past the trees. They were loaded with carbines, and one had an officer's belt and sword.

"Tomorrow the big army will feel our cannon guns in the other trap," he boasted.

Skulking from one bit of cover to another, waiting, crawling, never weakening his skill by wondering whether he would get away or not, Rafe Winburn finally got clear.

And now he was limping in open country in bright moonlight. He had a story to tell Old Stub.

On the plain beside the winding South Platte, moonlight spilled silver between the campfires of the largest army ever brought into the mountains. It made the horse herd restless; they were securely picketed and double guarded, and the troopers who had drawn the duty grumbled to each other about the senselessness of all the extra work. The moonlight gave outer sentries a feeling of unrealness as they tramped their posts. Some complained that their suppers had upset their stomachs, not realizing that the eerie light was disturbing their sense of balance.

For Infantryman Billy Munro, of Cincinnati, moonlight brought the mountains closer. It made them bigger and put them higher in the sky. They also made him feel colder. You sweat like sixty walking in the daytime, and then you bake one side while the other freezes standing around a fire at night.

"How do the Indians keep warm out here?" he asked.

"They ain't hardly human," Johannes said. Back to the fire, hands crossed behind him, he kept rubbing and twisting his wrists to keep them from becoming too hot in one place. "Wait till one of 'em rolls you out of your blankets tonight and screeches 'Coup!' in your ear." He grinned at a regular wearing distinctive stripes won in the Oregon Campaigns of '65-'68.

"Aw the devil," Munro said. He looked at campfires all around him, felt the stir of thousands of his kind. "To the devil with you, Johannes! A screeching Indian wouldn't be any worse than the racket you make tearing the lining out of your nose snoring."

Men laughed. Johannes grinned. "Some of these two-year boys might be all right yet."

Dan Beavers came slouching toward them. He reached inside his tunic and began to pass out biscuits still hot from the oven. Johannes shook his head. "Best forager I ever seen. He could've kept me fat in the war."

The Oregon campaigner held a biscuit in his mouth while he used both hands to pull the hot fronts of his pants legs away from the flesh beneath. He tried to talk before his mouth was free, then took the biscuit from his teeth. "Ain't no officer's blood on these, are there?"

Beavers grinned. "Only had to kill one major, and he fell away from the biscuits."

Johannes munched contentedly. "What's Old Stub fretting about tonight?"

Beavers turned his back to the fire. "One of the headquarters sergeants tells me he's still vaporing about no couriers from Freeland."

"He's just doing like he always does," Johannes said. "If I was Old Stub, I'd've left Freeland behind to nurse the sick ones. That's about all he's good for."

They ate their biscuits and listened to the sentries calling posts. It was fine, Billy Munro thought, to be a part of all this. Even if he never did get to shoot at an Indian, he'd have lots of things to tell when he got home.

He was in his blankets long before trumpeters sent their notes scattering over the tents, across the moonlit plain and toward the darker thickets on the skirts of the bright mountains.

Billy Munro slept well.

Old Stub's shadow was big behind him on sloping canvas as he stood before a field desk and looked at his division commanders and the officers they had brought with them. The general's hair was thin and wispy. It might have been any shade of brown once. There was vitality in the jut of his short gray beard, in the quick fixing and penetration of his long, dark eyes.

"Sit down, gentlemen," he said.

Two grizzled mountain men plumped quickly on the general's cot. They were relaxed and waiting several moments before the seven officers got adjusted in folding canvas chairs.

Short and wide, his rumpled uniform fitting loosely, Old Stub slowly rubbed the back of his legs against the edge of the field desk. His dark eyes moved from face to face. Quick as they were, they didn't dart; they bored for a moment in one place and then moved on to bore again.

His voice was harsh with a New England twang. "For at least the last two days we should have had couriers from General Freeland. We've had none. This army has sent three men a day to him for three days. Our communications still do not exist." The dark eyes went from one officer to another. "Our couriers to and from camp and the relay stations we've established behind us have not been molested." He let them think a moment. "Well?"

Arms folded on his barrel chest, dark-jowled Major-General Gross opened his eyes wide as he always did when speaking. The misty, pale-blue orbs seemed to push out beyond his fleshy nose. "Besides the Indians snapping up our messengers, do we have any reason to believe that Freeland isn't proceeding as planned?" Gross's words were spoken clearly and pronounced carefully, but they didn't escape the stubborn drag of his German heritage.

"No information has been withheld!"

Old Stub's gruffness was a little quicker and harsher than normal. It laid tension on the officers, even those who had known how worried he was. Scared to death! Major-General Montell thought.

Gross's strong right arm, Cavalry Colonel Jed Accola, crossed his legs and clasped long hands around one knee. His lean back was ramrod-erect. "Two days ago our scouts couldn't find an Indian in the area. You think now they're so thick riders can't get through to Freeland?"

"Where are the couriers?" Old Stub asked. For a moment they expected him to go into a crisp, familiar theme: "Gentlemen, communications are the heart of success in any military endeavors. From the bawl of the corporal to the order that moves twenty divisions . . ."

Old Stub looked at each of them. "I have a feeling that it would take a brigade of cavalry to reach Freeland."

The officers stared. Some of the younger men threw

quick sidewise glances at each other. From Old Stub's cot two scouts watched keenly, one of them gently moving his lower jaw. At his desk in one corner Lieutenant Collins, slender, neat, with long yellow mustache, wrote rapidly in beautiful script.

"I'm considering turning this army south within two hours—" the general smiled thinly—"to establish communications with General Freeland."

Gross seemed to settle into a big blue lump on an overloaded chair. His eyebrows came down, almost colorless in contrast to the blue-black of his jowls. Sitting there with his eyes half closed, Major-General Gross gave the appearance of a stupid, stubborn fat man.

Not at all like Major-General Armand Montell, whose broad, smooth brow and hard black eyes gave an impression of high intelligence and great drive. Montell was tall and gray, gray in the little pockets under his eyes, gray where lean cheeks were beginning to sag. Louisianian by birth, Montell had entered the Union forces as a colonel after the Confederacy refused him a higher rank—specifically that of supreme commander of Southern armies. After that the whole Civil War had become a poorly handled military mess, scarcely worth leaving the quartermaster general's office to investigate. Buying Southern cotton had been profitable, of course —about the only worthwhile activity of the war, Montell thought.

The untidy old peasant standing by the desk was a fussy hen, frightened when there was no hawk in sight. What had he been at West Point? A mathematical drudge, always getting punished for his careless appearance; but he, Armand Montell, had been the best fencer in his class, the best rider, a Cadet sergeant and a leader.

"Surely a few couriers stupid enough to be killed or captured by savages—" Montell spread his hands. His sneer sat in its familiar, delicate grooves. He had practiced it before uttering his first birth cries.

"That and other things," Old Stub said. "I want you to listen to Babcock and Phillips." His eyes rested a moment on the two scouts sitting on his cot, and for just an instant the general seemed undecided. "Bear in mind commands that have been mauled because some leader thought he knew more about a strange country than the men who lived in it."

Montell glanced carelessly at the scouts. It was bad enough to have civilians at this meeting without being insulted by a lecture from them. Those two uncouth louts . . . One of them was actually chewing tobacco right now!

"Go ahead, Babcock," Old Stub said.

The mountain man rose, long arms hanging awkwardly from slightly stooped, sloping shoulders. His salt-and-pepper beard was roughly trimmed. He walked to the door and spat an immense stream of tobacco juice near the legs of a startled sentry. Some of the officers swung around to look at him. Montell's face showed pure disgust.

"Well—" Babcock said.

Old Stub smiled. "Up here by the desk, Tobe."

There was nothing awkward about the scout as he went around one flank and stood before the desk, but immediately he choked up once more. "Well—"

Lieutenant Collins looked up, pen still against the paper. One "well" was quite enough, he thought, even if Old Stub was a fiend for exact reports.

Babcock rubbed his palms against the sides of his parfleche pants. "Well—"

Collins smiled faintly. So far the scout's report read like the talk of a man trying to work up interest in the boasting of a brand-new father.

"It's like this," Babcock said. He thought a while. "Today I find where five, six Indians been having target practice on a big piece of quartz."

He was silent. He looked helplessly at Old Stub.

"Go on, Tobe," the general said.

"Well—" Babcock rubbed his pants again—"that means the Indians got ammunition. The reason most of 'em, except the Nez Percé and some of them northern tribes, never could shoot a lick is because they never had more'n a few shells at one time. Now they got enough to practice. I don't say how good they're shooting—but they got spare ammunition."

Montell smiled. "Five or six of them, at least."

Babcock looked at Old Stub, conveying a desire to drop the whole matter and get on with his chewing.

"I'll amplify that in a moment," the general said. "Tell them what you told me this evening, Tobe." Old Stub studied his officers.

Babcock glared at Montell, selecting him as the man to convince. Montell smiled with the air of one humoring an idiot.

"I got a feeling these mountains is lousy with more Indians nor ever got together anywhere," the scout said. "I only seen a few signs—but you can feel it—" He spread his hands and frowned. "Well, it's just in the air—the way things feel . . . You can just feel it!"

Gross's eyes were almost closed. Colonel Accola's clean-shaven brown face was quiet and thoughtful. Montell's sneer was in full, delicate bloom. The rest of the group showed various degrees of polite interest or doubt.

T. T. Hickaman, stub-whiskered cavalry brigadier, asked gently: "You didn't—ah—*feel* how *many* Indians, did you?"

"They're here!" Babcock said. He glanced at Old Stub, then walked to the cot and sat down hard, glaring at his feet in the manner of one who has made a fool of himself with the co-operation of others.

"I credit Babcock's observation with bearing a good deal heavier on the situation than some of you gentlemen seem to think," Old Stub said. "We know that a good many of our supply trains have been captured, some of them freighting guns and ammunition exclusively. How many arms have been taken we don't know." He smiled at Montell. "Even if the telegraph were still operating, or the trains, I doubt that some of our quartermaster gentlemen could unravel the various contracts and other details enough to keep us informed."

Montell showed no trace of how bitterly he resented the reference to his former assignment.

"But we don't know that this talk of an Indian confederation is true—or partly true," Hickaman said.

Old Stub nodded. He looked at the second scout. "Let's hear from you, Phillips."

Geore Phillips was shorter by six inches than his partner. His eyes were small-set and gray, and in their flashing intensity they resembled Old Stub's. Three smallpox pits in the form of a tiny triangle lay in his forehead just above his left eye.

Phillips had no trouble speaking. "Today I find a few grains of parched corn. It were that little Indian kind, and there ain't none growed in these mountains. It looked like it come from a way-ee south."

Gross's expression made him look like a man brooding in fierce anger.

"It might be from Navajos or Pimas or Apaches," Phillips said. "Anyway, it's a long ways from home."

"Perhaps the Utes or Cheyennes raided down south and carried some back," Hickaman said.

"Yep! That might be." Phillips looked at Old Stub. "Ain't no use to say any more, is there?"

The general smiled. "No, that will do. Thank you, gentlemen."

The scouts went out. Those inside could hear Babcock expectorating with noisy vigor just after he passed through the opening.

Old Stub's quick eyes went over the group. "We've heard reports—rumor again—that Mescaleros and Lipans drove two large herds of stolen cattle up here to feed the other Indians."

"*All* we know is rumor!" a major said.

The general nodded. "It's what we don't know that makes things look ominous. There was a time when we could get Indians to carry information against each other like tattletale schoolboys. Those days are gone. Even the last of our Pawnee scouts are gone, scared completely out after word got around about the four of them that other Indians crucified on the Little Owyhee last fall.

"We lack accurate figures on the amount of equipment lost in the first campaigns and from supply trains that have been captured lock, stock and barrel. We may be up against a very large body of Indians as well armed as we. You who have faced a Sioux charge must have thanked God—I did, I assure you—that they were poorly armed. Today we know that the Indians have taken a good many of our own Springfield rifles. In one case that we do have figures we know they captured two thousand repeating carbines. They have taken light artillery, howitzers and Gatlings—"

to a breastwork defended by two worn Napoleons with mismatched wheels and no gunner's tools.

Old Stub recalled Trevarthen. He considered sending Montell, since Montell had given a wonderful demonstration of political skill during the war. However, the former quartermaster had spoken openly of the uselessness of taking artillery to subdue Indians. He had spoken of infantry in the same vein. A brigade of cavalry, Montell said, was quite sufficient.

So Old Stub sent a major to keep working on the Power. Two weeks later the army moved toward the mountains—without artillery. Still Old Stub hadn't given up entirely. He left orders with Colonel Nelson at Camp Pike to keep the army informed—just in case the major wrought a miracle and jarred loose a few pieces of artillery. It was a forlorn hope, but at least a hope.

Now, here in the tent beside the South Platte, Old Stub pulled his mind away from artillery he didn't have.

"Unless I hear some good reasons for following our original plan, tonight we're going south to find Freeland."

"But a few grains of corn, a few Indians shooting at a rock—even the loss of couriers—" Hickaman shook his head. "I don't think, sir, those are enough reasons to warrant changing our route."

"They might be," Gross said. His eyes went wide and bulged out. "The fact that six scouting parties that tried to cross the mountains didn't come back indicates there may be all the Indians here we've been hearing about. If so, they would naturally attack the smaller force. I say move tonight."

"Freeland has three thousand cavalry," Montell said. "Enough to club to death all the Indians in the world."

"He has a thousand infantry too," Colonel Accola said

drily. "But to club an Indian to death, first you catch him."

Gross chuckled deep in his throat. Montell shot him a look of detached scorn. Hickaman, who shared Montell's view of Old Stub, had begun another protest when a sun-tanned, gangling lieutenant stepped past the tent flap. Old Stub read the lieutenant's face and said, "Just a moment, Hickaman."

The officers swung around to look at the lieutenant.

"A courier just came through from General Freeland, sir!" The lieutenant had held his salute just the right length of time.

Old Stub grunted. "Well!"

"Yes, sir!" The lieutenant saluted again and ducked through the tent entrance.

The man who entered a few moments later was without hat or tunic. Both knees of his trousers and the woolens beneath were gone, and bloody flesh showed in the rents. The left sleeve of his gray shirt was ripped off at the shoulder seam. The blood-soaked woolen underwear of that arm had been slit to make a bandage around the heavy muscles above his elbow. His shirt was ripped and bloody down the front. His face was tired. Dust lay thick on his short dark hair, and the whites of his eyes showed bloodshot under the lanterns hanging from the center pole of the tent.

"Corporal Thompson, Company K, Fourth—"

"Where's Freeland?" Old Stub asked.

The messenger seemed to have trouble shifting thought in full flight. "Why—just above the South Fork of the Arkansas when I left at noon yesterday, sir."

"All right?"

"Yes, sir. The scouts and the advance party have been skirmishing a little with Indians. That's all, sir."

Old Stub knocked two map cases to the ground as he sat down on his desk. "Go ahead with the message, Corporal."

"General Freeland requests reason for having had no communications and says he is proceeding to the meeting place as planned." The courier swayed a little.

"No written dispatch?" Old Stub asked.

"Lieutenant Bass had it, sir. The other two of us knew the message."

Colonel Accola relaxed, as though brutally tired. Bass had been from his own home town in Illinois. The lieutenant had come by to say hello when he'd reported at Camp Pike.

Old Stub nodded, his dark eyes studying the courier. The corporal was young, rangy, clean-cut, with dark-blue eyes that showed a hint of wildness, which would have to level off before the lad could get along well with men under him. Still, he was the first messenger to make the ride between the armies. The least a man could do would be to make a sergeant of him. He looked at the courier's bandaged arm and the blood on his torn shirt.

"You must know why couriers haven't been getting through," the general said.

The reckless light heightened in the corporal's eyes. He started to smile, caught himself. "Yes, sir."

"Did you encounter any large body of them?" Old Stub asked.

"No, sir. Just plenty to give three men trouble. I finished on one of their horses."

Old Stub nodded. "Bullet in the arm?"

"Arrow, sir. Only one of the bunch that got after us in the rocks had a gun. Sounded like an old smoothbore."

Montell's sneer became just a trifle more apparent.

He looked at those around him and nodded gently.

Old Stub didn't raise his voice when he called. The lieutenant popped through the tent opening. "Take Corporal Thompson to the surgeon. Take care of him otherwise. Have him back here in an hour. Have Babcock and Phillips, the two scouts, here also." He looked from Montell to Gross as the courier and the lieutenant left. "We will move on tomorrow, according to plan."

The officers rose. Tension eased. Lieutenant Collins wrote happily in his corner. There was nothing worrisome about the written word: once you had it down it was trapped, available and unchanging.

Montell said to Hickaman, "We'll have to get in a little antelope hunting when the terrible threat abates. With all the Indians supposed to be lurking about you'd think game would be scarcer, wouldn't you?"

Old Stub didn't hear. He was sitting at his desk, tugging at a map case. If one worry had lifted from his mind another had replaced it so quickly that his expression hadn't changed at all.

"Good night, gentlemen," he said absently.

The officers went out.

Old Stub studied a map. According to it and the courier's information, Freeland was at least a full day's march ahead of schedule. That was odd, since the messenger said he had encountered no large bodies of Indians. Still, Freeland was a driver when he was on the move, a driver with a tendency to seek trouble a little too readily.

A full report from Corporal Thompson might help clarify things. If Freeland wanted to move his scouting force at high speed that was all right. What Old Stub wanted to know most was whether or not Corporal

Thompson had encountered Indians from several different tribes.

Babcock and Phillips would know from the description.

Waning moonlight left brightness only on the white summits of the mountains, losing power over increasing blackness in timber and in rock hollows and in the aspen thicket where Iron Buffalo lay on his robes, grateful to be at last away from the endless boastings and orations of the giant council.

The herbs bound smoking hot in soft buckskin felt good around his knee. Without moving his head he looked at She Who Rides, his only wife, sitting on the other side of the tiny lodge fire. Her tongue was like her father's, old Fighting Bear, now asleep in his robes by the west wall. And, like the old man, she spoke only after thought, though often the words stirred dark questions in Buffalo's heart.

He was tired from the long counciling. It was hard to sit quietly and listen to foolish talk and not be able to rise straight up and say: "We will do this!" If he just once said that, though many of the young men, even some from strange tribes, would shout with him and be ready to follow, the other chiefs would stand from him and say later in their lodges: "Iron Buffalo does not council. He is like the white man, speaking his own name many times, saying we must do as he plans and no other way."

At best the Indians were restless, wanting to leave soon for their own lands, not trusting each other. When this was so it was hard to sit for long and listen to foolish things said by cowards; to keep one's face always like a stone; then to rise and speak and win your way slowly by praising here, rebuking there—not too strongly—sometimes by asking for much advice from the Big Belly chiefs, many of whom held strong desires for peace.

This was the Indians' way, often making one growl inside when those whose words were but wind through the trembling trees spoke long. Even so, this way was good. No chief could say what any Indian had to do. The chiefs could say what they thought was best, and if they spoke with strong, wise hearts others might follow them.

Iron Buffalo remembered two soldiers he had seen on the walking place at Laramie. They held their rifles over their heads in both hands, running and running while a little sub-chief of the soldiers watched. They ran until they fell from weariness and lay on the ground like dead. This foolish thing they had been made to do because one of the big soldier chiefs had so ordered it.

The Indians' way was better. But it was long.

Many times the council had been interrupted. Only a part of the young men had been in the fighting when the foolish soldier chief sent some of his riding soldiers up a narrow place. Those who had missed the fighting had been wild to ride at once and steal the horses of the big army by night. The chiefs had stopped this foolish thing before it could start. But though the *akicita* worked hard to hold the young men, many of them slipped away to join the fighting with the second part of the little army.

Even the Big Bellies, who had seen soldier chiefs do very foolish things, had grunted in surprise when three Blackfeet messengers came after dark to say that some Cheyennes had led many of the riding soldiers into a trap.

"Like the antelope they tumbled into the trap," one of

the Blackfeet said, waving a many-shooting gun he had taken. "All are dead!"

Though the Blackfeet had long been enemies of the Tetons and not to be trusted even though they had taken the pipe, Iron Buffalo saw they spoke good words from strong hearts, and gave each of them one of his best ponies, though he had few to spare.

Later, Crooked Arm and Little Howling Wolf, two of Iron Buffalo's Oglala followers, came riding fast to say the same as the Blackfeet. Crooked Arm and Little Howling Wolf had been for days with the Sioux and Cheyennes, who watched for and killed all messengers between the armies.

"One of the hairy-faced old scouts escaped after killing Bull Elk, who had shot the white man from his horse at the very first of the fighting," Crooked Arm reported. "The young men are following his tracks, but they were very late in starting because it was long after the fighting before we found Bull Elk lying dead in the thick berry trees, and saw where the white man had crawled away."

"You have done well in carrying the message," Iron Buffalo said. He gave away two more ponies.

While a Gros Ventre chief boasted in council of his people's might, Iron Buffalo thought about the news. It was not good. He had not planned to fight the little army until after the Indians had fought the big one. He had hoped to hold the little army, to delay it until after the big fighting was done. Now, if the hairy-faced old guide escaped to tell, the big army would be warned and could not be surprised.

Still it was done now, and perhaps the young men would catch the guide. But Iron Buffalo knew that those hairy-faced old ones who had lived long in the mountains were not easy to catch.

Then the tattooed ones, Arapaho, came riding to say that those who had killed part of the little army in the antelope trap had ridden fast and were fighting with the other part led by the soldier chief called Freeland. They had caught him in another rocky place that led from the valley, not like the first place, but still among rocks where the Indians could fight well. One of the old mountain men had seen the Indians before all the army got into the bad place. Even so the warriors had trapped part of the soldiers, forcing the rest into the rocks farther down the valley. And now much fighting was still going on, even with the light gone.

Iron Buffalo said nothing. It was hard to hold these young warriors. They had spoiled many good traps before, and now they might have done it again. But it was done. The young men shook their rifles over their heads and called for Iron Buffalo to lead them, so that when light came they could finish all the soldiers from the second part of the little army.

Iron Buffalo kept his face like a rock. "Let the young men already there take care of the fighting. These little armies are nothing. Iron Buffalo and the older chiefs will wait for the big fighting against the one called Old Stub."

Some of the older chiefs could not conceal their thinking well. They looked at Iron Buffalo with their mouths showing like one who eats much air. The little armies were as nothing! Never before had they even heard of any army as large as the big one. And yet Iron Buffalo spoke as one talking of a buffalo hunt.

So great was the shouting and laughing of the young warriors that much time passed before the council could go on. Through it all Iron Buffalo knew that some of the Big Bellies were filled with fear over this thing that had been done, but now that the fighting had started they would think well before speaking against it.

Even so, many did speak against more fighting, some saying that it would be best to go quickly from the mountains, returning to their own lands, scattering so that no one could say who had been in the fighting. Some said it would be wise to send strong men to tell those still fighting to let the soldiers go in peace. Now that the white men had seen that the Indians could fight together as brothers and had felt their power, the soldiers would go away, sending men with gifts to talk of peace; asking what the Indians wanted instead of telling them what they could have. Many of the older chiefs made the approving grunts, but their eyes moved a little toward Iron Buffalo. They knew what he would say; they wondered how he would say it.

In the great council were many little chiefs, who in ordinary times would not be sitting there; but the wise old men and Iron Buffalo, too, said it was better to have little chiefs sitting under the great sky of buffalo hides, feeling power, than to have them outside with blackness growing in their hearts. Much trouble might rise from little things, the wise ones said. Little tribes with few warriors were often brothers of large tribes with many warriors. Strike one of the few, strange-tongued Sarsi and you would be injuring a Blackfoot; insult a Delaware and you had insulted all the Shawnees.

Face to the Storm, the Delaware, spoke well, standing in his robes of twisted rabbit skin, a gift from Thunder Elk, great leader of the Nez Percé. Face to the Storm had been for many years an interpreter for soldiers on the plains. He had been so long among white men he could read their many little signs on paper.

"When I brought my few people with our brothers

the Shawnee, some of us were lean from hunger, some swelled from white man's whisky, some wearing clothing the soldiers had thrown away. We have been given food. We have been given robes. We are among friends. Our hearts are grateful.

"Some say the white man will go back. Some say he will leave the western tribes their land." He raised both hands to the sky. "My people were once as the fires above, with much land and great forests near the salt waters far to the east. The white man came. Now we are few, and would be none if it were not for our brothers the Shawnees.

"I am not old, not fifty as the white man counts. Yet for every year of my life there is a treaty with my people that the white men have broken." Face to the Storm made the signs for forty-five. "That many times has the white man made solemn promises in council. That many times has he lied and cheated my people. Today we are few, far from the lands we owned. The white men say because we left we have no rights. The white men drove us from our lands. Now he says we should have stayed.

"We will go no farther toward the setting sun. We will die here fighting if we must."

In silence the Delaware sat down.

Cuerno spoke next. He was the brother of Arrow Flying Far, leader of the Utes who had been strong for peace with the white men. When Huajatola, Black Indian war chief, and most of the young men went to war, Arrow Flying Far had taken his lodge far into the mountains and would not come. Cuerno had come, but his heart was dark with thinking about the bad thing that had been done to his brother.

"I say for our brothers to go back to their homes. Our young men have killed many soldiers this day. The

Great White Father will think long about what has been done this day. He will see that it was a bad thing to send soldiers after us. He will know that we are strong and he will treat us now as one strong warrior treats another, with honor. The Utes have had little trouble with the white men. We have sold land, and they have kept their promises.

"We have fought today. I do not say that it was wrong. But now the game is getting very scarce from so many of our brothers being here. We are glad to give our brothers our game. But after they have returned to their lands we must live here yet. My heart says it would be best to take our victories and our dead and go to our homes. Let the big army wear its moccasins out looking for those who are not here. Then it will go away."

Many grunted loudly in approval when the big dark chief of the Black Indians sat down.

Others spoke, and then it was Iron Buffalo's time to make words. Some of the Oglala and Cheyennes started a fight, each side claiming that Iron Buffalo was more theirs than the others', though it was known that his father had been a famous Cheyenne Dog warrior and his mother an Oglala, one of the few women who had made the Sun Dance with the warriors.

The *akicita* of many tribes used their clubs well, and soon the fighting was stopped.

Iron Buffalo knew he must not say too much, as the Big Bellies always did, and yet enough to make his listeners believe.

"I have heard our brothers. They have seen many years and are wise. They are wiser than Iron Buffalo. He only knows what is in his heart. He only knows the things he has seen in the holy dreams. Some of the chiefs say that we should go home now, pretending that we are at peace with the white man, pretending that there are no blue soldiers lying dead and scalped in the narrow place between the rocks.

"I do not say the old chiefs are wrong. I say they have forgotten. Their memories are short. They have forgotten the white man's peace with our brothers at Sand Creek. They have forgotten the Unkpatilas who went to talk of peace with the white soldiers, our brothers who were stabbed from the back with the long gun-knives of the soldiers and then hung from ropes before the fort.

"They have forgotten what Face to the Storm has said. The white man continues to take our land and kill our brother the buffalo even when he says he will not do so. The soldiers will not forget the fighting this day. Their Great Chief in Washington will not forget, though he never comes to fight himself or see that those who make promises keep their word. If we go back to our homes now the soldiers will kill our helpless ones wherever they can find them.

"They will begin with the Utes, in whose country the fighting today started. Our brother Cuerno will not have to feel sad about the game. There will be no Utes to eat it. We cannot fight in little bands. Together we can do much. With the trap we have made we can fight the big army even as the little one. Many buffalo are sometimes more foolish and easier to kill than one small herd with wise-watching bulls."

Iron Buffalo saw that even some of the Big Bellies were forgetting fear.

"Before every one of our brothers the buffalo is but a skull looking toward the dying sun on the Shining Mountains; before we are hunted like the Delawares;

before our lands are taken by those who dig the earth to plant, by those who make our rivers muddy in their search for the yellow dirt; before our helpless ones are killed and the last of our young men lie drunk around the soldier forts and agencies—Iron Buffalo will be dead, too. Iron Buffalo will be dead because he will charge the big army all alone before he lets it go from these mountains untouched."

Iron Buffalo's voice was low, but so silent were the Indians his words went far into the night, above the quiet trees, even beyond the smoke-browned tops of the few lodges of women who had been allowed to come from the big camp behind the mountains.

One of the Modocs far from his land near the big western waters, knowing but little of Dakota speech, but with a strong heart, raised his voice like thunder.

"Hoka hey!" he shouted.

The roar of voices made a stirring in the sky of buffalo skins above the great council. Trees trembled with the shouting. Still Cuerno and some of the others were cold inside. But they would fight, Iron Buffalo knew. They went where the people went.

Now the long counciling was over.

Lying on his robes Iron Buffalo watched the quiet face of She Who Rides. He would have talked to her, but he knew what she would say. Though she was strong of heart, even having done the Sun Dance like her mother, she was still a woman with peace in her heart and fear for the helpless ones, even when she led Iron Buffalo's war ponies to him and said: "Go!"

He moved his leg a little as the pack around his knee began to cool. She Who Rides dipped more herbs on a piece of skin, taking them with a wooden spoon from the stone kettle with the heated rocks inside. She bound new heat around his leg. It chased the pain, but still Iron Buffalo could not sleep, thinking of the things to come.

Those who had seen the fighting today said the young men had been strong, not doing foolish things to get killed. If Crooked Arm's young men caught the old hairy-faced one, and if none of the soldiers had escaped to tell the big army, the soldier chief called Old Stub would not be expecting a battle. Still, he was not a fool. Iron Buffalo had seen him on the plains before the white men's war among themselves, and the little soldier chief did not have the eyes of a foolish one.

But would the warriors fight as well as they had today? Many of them had not had a chance to kill the little army, but it would take all the warriors to make battle against the big one. Indians soon grew tired of fighting, wanting to boast and dance and feast. It was hard for them to know that war on the white man was not like riding far to take a few scalps and steal a few ponies, running away fast if the enemy was too strong, then forgetting until the next raid.

Would they forget about the sun signals from the old men watching on the hills where they could see much that those fighting could not see? Would they lose time from killing to count coup?

There were many questions in Iron Buffalo's heart. Cold as the blizzard that howls around the lodge in the Moon of Popping Trees, stilling even the talking of the women, was the sureness that he would ride to let the soldiers kill him if the warriors did not fight well or became afraid and ran away.

He wondered if the Oglalas he had sent to catch the white man whom the Crows slyly called Eats People had found him yet. They were not to kill Eats People, because it would make the Crows angry to know that Sioux had killed one who lived among the Crows, even a white man who ate people, even a white man with a heart so black he had showed Indians how to use cannon guns to kill his own people.

So after the great council, when the boy came riding from the women's camp over the mountains to say that Eats People had sneaked away, Iron Buffalo sent only older warriors who would not act in black anger without thought when they caught the white man. If Eats People was killed, the Crows would say that he was not riding to tell the soldiers about the cannon guns. Maybe he wasn't, Iron Buffalo thought, but it would be best not to let the white man have a chance to tell.

It was a heavy thing to keep peace among so many Indians. After the fiighting they would scatter quickly, and that was good. If they won they would come more readily when it was time to fight again.

She Who Rides rose quickly when they heard a pony coming fast. Then someone was walking toward the lodge, wetting his moccasins in the morning dew, for time was moving toward the light again.

The scratching on the hide came quick and sharp. She Who Rides opened the flap. Tall Bad Jaw entered. Bad Jaw had saved Iron Buffalo's life twice. Once when the strong Unkpatila had ridden close to the wagons before Julesburg to lift the wounded Iron Buffalo from the ground; again in the fighting of last summer on Bow River.

"The second fighting goes well," Bad Jaw said. "Not like in the steep place, but good."

Iron Buffalo started to rise, but from the shadows behind him She Who Rides put a strong hand on his shoulder. Bad Jaw pretended not to see.

"Did the young men forget the signaling?" Iron Buffalo asked.

"They remembered well, even after the sun's going, when old chiefs sitting high in the rocks used fire. Many of the riding soldiers got away and went down the valley, but Kiowas and Comanches and others met them and drove them into the rocks."

Old Fighting Bear peered from his robes. "How many of our young men have been killed?"

"Many," Bad Jaw said.

Silence ran in the lodge for the flight of a duck across a small lake.

"Did the soldiers do a foolish thing, like those who rode into the antelope trap?" Iron Buffalo asked.

"They did not wait to cross the wide pass where the guides had said. Their chief, Freeland, chose another place, saying that the picture writing showed it was closer. It was not a good place."

"How do you know what you say?" Fighting Bear asked.

Bad Jaw's face was dark and bleak in the poor light. "I found among the rocks a wounded guide. It was he who saved our few lodges by warning of the soldiers' coming when we were peaceful many moons ago on Powder River. He told me."

Fighting Bear waited. She Who Rides was motionless in the shadows, but her eyes were straight on Bad Jaw.

"In all the fighting I could not get him away," Bad Jaw said. "His leg moved sidewise from his horse's falling from a bullet. I left him my *wasna* and hid him carefully in a coyote home among the rocks, covering the hole with bushes. When light comes I will send old men and ponies to get him away."

"By then the Black Indians or the Apaches from the

south will have him," old Fighting Bear said quietly. "Tell me now where he is and I will go, not waiting for the light. Fighting Bear was in the lodges of the Unkpatilas on Powder River when this man told us of the soldiers' coming in the night to kill our helpless ones."

She Who Rides went from the lodge.

Fighting Bear rose from his robes and dressed, wishing that he had his warm green and white *capote,* taken from a Crow he'd scalped two years before. But since the tribes had taken the pipe Fighting Bear had told his wife to keep the *capote* away from sight in the parfleche bundle. It would have been better to have burned it, but there would be days again when the Crows were not friends . . .

He listened well to Bad Jaw as he dressed. Then the old man walked into the night. She Who Rides was already bringing two ponies for him.

"You did a good thing, my brother," Iron Buffalo said. "This white man has a good heart, even if he does ride with the soldiers." He sat up. Firelight gleamed dully on his scarred breast.

"He was the one who saw us in the rocks and warned the soldiers," Bad Jaw said.

"Still it was a good thing you did."

They heard She Who Rides and Fighting Bear talking in low voices.

"What of the young white man called Sunfish? Was he at the fighting?" Iron Buffalo asked.

For the white man with the short, dark hair Iron Buffalo felt nothing but scorn. He was one of four who had dug by a northern river, four who had sneaked back after the Indians told them to go. When they were caught this young one spoke up straight, asking to be taken with the Indians. For all the little sacks of yellow stones and dirt the other three had the young one said he would go among the soldiers and tell the Indians what they were planning.

Iron Buffalo's warriors wanted to kill him with the rest, even though they saw he was not afraid in his asking. They wondered why the white man, for a few sacks of yellow dirt, would want to sneak among his own people like a Crow hiding in the women's lodges.

Iron Buffalo knew. When he was young he had seen two white men kill another for just a little of the yellow dirt. Then Iron Buffalo had killed both the others, and had been angry when he saw they had nothing but yellow dirt in the sack. He had been so disgusted he hadn't They wondered why the white man, for a few sacks of worthless earth into the river. But when he grew older he had learned better.

He did not let the young men kill the white man. Nor did he let them throw away the sacks of heavy earth. Though his heart was black with scorn he had agreed to let the young white man come with them. The others who dug by the river shouted at the young one in great anger, calling him many times "Sunfish!" And that was how he was known by the Indians.

"Sunfish was at the first fighting with us," Bad Jaw said. "He did not shoot against his people. After it was done he took the clothing of a dead soldier who had fought well. He bruised his own knees with stones. From one of the Striped Arrow people I took a bow and shot the white man in the arm. He laughed and bound it, tearing some of the soldier clothing. Then he rode to tell the chief of the big army that only a few Indians with poor guns were in the mountains."

Iron Buffalo did not show his thoughts. True, this Sunfish, whose eyes grew mad at the sight of the yellow dirt, had gone once to the big soldier camp and had come back with truth in his words. But now that he had seen his people killed, his heart might change and he might tell about the guns, even as Eats People had gone to do. And Eats People had been many years among the Crows, living like them, being taken into a warrior society, but still his heart had been with his own people.

Iron Buffalo did not blame the two white men. He did wish now that he had let the Indians kill Sunfish with the other three, and that he had left someone to guard Eats People.

But it was done. Iron Buffalo was angry in his heart, yet he did not want to rebuke a brother.

"For doing this thing Sunfish wanted three more sacks of the yellow stones," Bad Jaw said. He read his brother's face. "His heart is filled with yellow stones, as your heart is filled with wanting to save our land and buffalo for the Indians, even ones who are our enemies. For that you would ride against the big army alone. When I came those watching the ponies told me. For what is in the heart of Sunfish he will speak to his own people with the crooked tongue. I say it, or I would not have let him go."

They were silent. Outside they heard Fighting Bear starting to ride away.

"You will never ride alone, my brother," Bad Jaw said to Iron Buffalo.

The words warmed the slender chief sitting on his robes so that he could not speak. He merely looked at the strong, solemn face of the tall Unkpatila, and felt the strong sun of friendship, which needs no words in any language.

All else Bad Jaw had said about Sunfish could be, Iron Buffalo admitted. Not long ago among his own people there had been many who sold themselves to white men for drink that killed the head and flour that made the stomach twist with worms. Sunfish had grown up without a father to walk with him and teach him the right ways; without a mother to love him and teach him to keep his voice low in the lodge and help those who needed help. From Sunfish Iron Buffalo had heard strange tales that among white men were children that no one wanted, little helpless ones left by their mothers. They were kept in big forts and fed all at once like soldiers making a long line before the cooking wagons, and no one wanted the little ones. The strange story might be true.

Iron Buffalo threw the cold herbs from his knee and rose naked from his robes. Gray light was sneaking around the lodge flap.

He looked at Bad Jaw. "This may be a good day to die."

Bad Jaw nodded grimly.

Outside in the cold false dawn She Who Rides stood in the wet grass watching old Fighting Bear riding away to help the white man who had saved the Unkpatila lodges in the long-ago days of peace.

But even then, she thought, there had not been peace.

Fighting Bear went from sight.

The sun at noon lay hot on lichen-gray granite in a little winding pass that led from the valley of the Upper Arkansas to the rolling antelope lands above. On Freeland's map the gulch had been a short cut.

Now it was a death trap.

Where shade still held on the rough north slopes a man lay in a coyote den, bearded face pressed close to bushes that had been bent to screen the entrance.

Firing in the little pass was dying slowly. Sounds of heavy fighting still came from somewhere down the valley, where seven hundred cavalrymen had been driven to dismount and take cover on a rock-strewn hill after failing to break through five times their weight of Comanches, Kiowas, Arapahos, Apaches and other Indians.

On the high pinnacles above the pass the sun winked from mirrors, telling creeping Indians in the rocks below where little pockets of resistance lay.

Oblivious to the scattered fighting around him Fighting Bear led his ponies slowly, searching the slopes, checking trees and odd-shaped rocks. Warriors crouched or sprawled behind cover glanced curiously at the exposed old Brule. Some shouted at him to get down. Most of them turned their heads away. It was not best to look too long on one searching for a dead son or nephew.

At last old Fighting Bear saw the place Bad Jaw had described. There were still too many warriors in the pass, though more and more were going away to where the heavier gunfire sounded. Fighting Bear sat down beside his ponies, shielded by a big granite block. He smoked his short stone pipe and watched the mirror signals from the high places. There would be time to help the white man, though by late afternoon Fighting Bear was supposed to be many miles away, using the gilt-framed mirror now in the hide sack on his spotted pony. If Fighting Bear, Iron Buffalo and Bad Jaw did not live to see another day, She Who Rides would not forget the white man who had saved the Unkpatila lodges.

The old Brule smoked and waited.

After a time the last sun-twinkling stopped on the high places; the last shot sounded in the pass; Indians went toward the other fight, some carrying several guns, all carrying many scalps. Old Fighting Bear thought scalps taken this way was too much like cutting them from the skins of buffalo driven over a cliff.

When the last screaming warrior had left the pools of blue that lay among the rocks, the Brule rose and led his ponies toward the coyote den. He called out softly from the side, saying the white man's name. There came a low, choked sound from within. Fighting Bear approached and pulled the bushes aside, first looking around to be sure that none was watching.

Some time, not long before, a glancing bullet had struck a rock near the entrance to the den, twisting, flying endwise and entering the white man's chest. The little cry he had made when Fighting Bear called had been but the choking gurgle of life coming from his throat. Perhaps the bullet had been from a soldier gun, perhaps from an Indian rifle. It didn't matter.

The white man was dead when Fighting Bear knelt beside him.

With tears running from his wrinkled face the old Brule piled many heavy stones before the entrance and rode away.

The noise of fighting from the other place was still loud as thunder in the mountains.

Pressed into dark mud under the arched tips of long grass beside a beaver dam on the South Platte, Rafe Winburn chewed hardtack that even water couldn't soften. Through the bending grass above him he read the sun as noon. He chewed and rested and waited.

By less than an hour he'd missed the army. The moon had been down when he saw the campfires. If the shadowy riders speaking Sioux in low tones had given him forty minutes more he could have reached an outpost.

Instead he'd had to lie low beside the stream. Now he thanked God that, before false dawn, he had rolled into the river and crawled down to where he could swim to concealment on the far side of a big beaver dam.

It had cost him his rifle. Otherwise it would have cost his life, for the Sioux searched patiently for him until light began to break. Then they rode to a far hill and watched from the aspens, waiting for him to make a break. And so he'd had to lie in chilling mud while the army came to life and moved on. Even half an hour more might have been enough.

The Indians on the hill were gone now, he was sure, but there would be others watching.

Winburn didn't curse his luck. He had had too much good fortune in staying alive thirty-five years in the mountains and on the plains. He knew that only incredible luck had brought him through the bright moonlit hours when he was walking in the open.

He gnawed his hardtack and waited. Night would come again.

Simon Bullard, known slyly among his brother Crows as Eats People, knew his sagging pony could not stand the gaff much longer. The six riders coming fast behind him would have him soon.

Oglala they were, he guessed by the way they rode. The big cream pony in the lead looked like White Beaver's, strong friend of Iron Buffalo. The worst he could expect from them would be a whipping with their war ropes. What he could expect from Iron Buffalo was a thought he didn't dwell on.

He showed his white heritage by cursing vilely when four ponies shot out of the aspens several hundred yards ahead on his right. They came skimming across the grassland to intercept him. He showed again that he was a white man by kicking his pony and riding on.

Then he cursed in joy. The four Indians ahead were Crows. He veered toward them, shouting. Big white teeth gleamed in his coal-black beard. He raised one arm in recognition.

The Crows came on.

One of the foremost riders called his name. "Bull-ard!"

Cannibal Bullard began talking when he was close enough to be heard, and that was far, for his voice was deep and strong.

"Teton! Oglala!" he bellowed. "Iron Buffalo sends them to kill me so he will not have to pay the ponies he promised!"

The lie, the appeal to ancient hatred was effective. His brother Crows closed around him protectively. Simon Bullard was fast in his cunning talk.

In a few seconds he was riding on. Behind him was a pony tired almost to exhaustion. It stood with trembling legs and drooping head among the Crows. They were beginning to look at each other a trifle uneasily. Bullard laughed and shouted: "Charge the Oglala!" Already his fresh horse was gaining in spite of his great weight.

He had a comfortable lead when he again looked back. The Oglala had reached the Crows. Arms were waving. Then the Sioux were coming on—and with them came the Crows. Bullard's big laugh rang out. He had chosen the best pony of the four. Ahead he saw an advance detail from a rolling dust cloud far beyond. If his brother Crows pressed too hard, his Spencer rifle would be the answer to brotherhood.

Great God! They were really bringing an army! They ought to give him some kind of reward, something better than ponies. Why hell, after all he was a *white* man!

The Crows' ponies were fresh, but the riders were losing heart the closer Bullard got to the advance detail. Then some of the soldiers came riding out to meet him. Still the Oglala pressed on, but their ponies were flagging.

He'd make it. A big reward in gold would be better than ponies and a life in a stinking lodge. But what if the Army had captured an Indian who had spilled his guts about who showed the Indians how to handle artillery? . . . Or what if some officer recognized him from that old court-martial! . . . It was an awful big army, and there might be men among it from his old artillery company.

Cannibal Bullard, known slyly among the Crows as Eats People, had one cold, clear thought: he wished to hell he had stayed in the women's camp behind the range and let the squaws jeer.

Behind him the Oglala were taking long shots in desperation. Ahead of him was an army. *The* Army. He had murdered twice while a member of it. An officer's memory was twice as long as an Indian's.

Cannibal Bullard had no choice at the moment. Wind riding through his curling black whiskers, noonday heat beating down on him, he went toward his own people.

Scouts Tobe Babcock and Geore Phillips slouched in their saddles and ate peaches from a tin can, spearing the dripping halves with broad-bladed knives that had been used at various times for such duties as trimming beards and toenails, skinning bears, cleaning fish, butchering deer and ripping the bellies of Indians who had misjudged the light sleeping habits of the pair.

They shared the juice from the can, used sleeves to smear the stickiness a little deeper into their beards and gave their knives a few sterilizing swipes across the rumps of their horses.

Three-quarters of a mile to their right the army was halted just short of a green valley between two purple mesas. Nothing but battle could keep Old Stub from feeding his men and horses at noon.

Babcock tossed the can over his shoulder and reached for chewing tobacco. "He warn't going to make the riffle till he switched ponies at that lead bunch. How do you figure that?"

Phillips shook his head. Under his flat Mormon hat his brow and eyes were puckered as he watched the rider streaking toward the advance detail. An Indian on a cream pony was still after him. As the scouts watched, troopers speared out from the advance detail. The Indian wheeled his pony and went back toward others who were waiting. The troopers gained, but they couldn't catch the pony riders before they reached the shelter of trees.

"He ain't no courier," Phillips said. "He rides like an Indian, and he's coming from the wrong direction."

For a while the scouts sat in silence, feeling the weight of the sun on their backs and shoulders.

"Whatever he is, they think he's important," Babcock observed. "The advance detail sent someone with him, and they're both flying their kites to get to the army."

"I can see a little yet, Tobe," Phillips grunted.

Babcock grinned. "Who was the first to see that courier last night had his hair chopped off with a knife instead of scissors?"

"Who was the first one to say he had an Indian smell on him?"

Babcock nodded. "I smelled him, too, but did you think I was going to say anything—even to Old Stub—after the way them idiots with stars and eagles laughed in my face about 'feeling' Indians?"

Phillips laughed so hard the pox pits above his left eye turned flaming red. "You can't smell 'em as far as *you* made out!"

"By God! You knowed what I meant!"

"Sure I did! But you should have drawed the picture some other way for them officers," Phillips said.

"Yeah! You didn't make such a hell of a stir talking about your corn, did you?"

Phillips watched until the two riders were lost somewhere in the outskirts of the army. His face was serious. "Outside of Old Stub hisself and that big German who bugs his eyes when he's talking, none of them officers would think there was Indians around if arrows started ripping through the tent!"

His chew well-seated, Babcock swung around to look keenly at aspen-covered ridges rising up and up toward blue timber on the mountains. "If Old Stub promised to make a colonel out of me, I wouldn't ride through them trees right now."

Phillips grinned. "You're still feeling Indians, huh?"

They rode on. Their eyes watched the trees and hills, read the ground before them, saw what there was to see. Their faces were sensitive to little changes in the wind. Their minds were ready to grasp quickly the details of any fast-rising threat they had faced before.

Between them they had the experience of seventy-eight years of hazardous living.

Cannibal Bullard rode with a corporal from the advance detail. He had already forgotten the narrow squeak of a short time before. Bullard's mind was busy with new problems. Would it be better to say first that he had some important information and ask what it was worth? Or should he talk and trust the general to do the right thing? A disquieting thought popped up. Would they expect him to tell all he knew about the Indians' plans just because he was a white man—and not even think he should be paid? What had the army ever done for him, besides trying to hang him?

The more he tried to handle his thoughts the surer he became that the white man's life he had forsaken seven years before was filled with many problems. Things had been lots simpler with the Crows.

Soldiers eating their cold biscuits and beans looked up curiously as the corporal rode past with this great black-bearded man in Indian braids. As in any group of armed men, their remarks were not gentle.

"Wasn't for the bastard's beard and them stary eyes, I'd say he was Indian, sure enough."

"Here's one redskin we scared out of the mountains!"

"How'd you like to suddenly meet *that* in the dark?"

And then a tall, red-faced cavalryman who had been a trapper and Indian trader after the Civil War stared hard at the Crows' white brother. "Hey, fellows! That's old Cannibal Bullard from way up north! Cannibal Bullard!"

"Cannibal!"

"Yeah! He et a dozen Indians one winter when they was all starving!"

"Cannibal! . . . cannibal! . . . ate humans! . . ." The words ran far ahead of the two riders. "Et his own half-breed kids! . . . Just as lief chew on a man's thigh-bone as a buffalo rib! . . . Cannibal! . . ."

Men jostled to get a close look at the monster.

At first Bullard cursed those who yelled insults at him. As the news ran on and more voices raised he became sullen. Goddam! he thought bitterly. None of them was ever starving like I was. Goddam them! Ain't I suffered enough, waking up in the night and thinking about that? Don't I know my mind ain't been right since then?

A fat-cheeked cavalry captain stopped the pair. "Where are you taking this man, Corporal?"

"To Old—to the general, sir. He has an important message."

"Who says it's important?" the captain demanded.

The corporal was a regular. His face became as stolid as an Iroquois ceremonial mask. "*He* does, sir."

"Take him to Colonel Accola, Gross' First Brigade. The general can't listen to every squaw man that comes along!"

Regulars who heard were silent. Some of the two-year men muttered and glared at the captain. "But, sir—" The corporal started to explain his first orders.

"Take him to Colonel Accola!" The captain rapped his words and spaced them far apart.

"Yes, sir." The corporal and Bullard rode on.

Terror blacker than his beard was rushing through Bullard. He no longer heard the jibes around him. He was looking down the years at a major with elbows resting on a table at a court-martial. "We are trying to be fair with you, Sergeant Bullard. Besides personal hatred, was there any other reason for killing your battery officer? Lieutenant Accola has testified . . ."

Lieutenant Accola . . . Colonel Accola . . . There was only one Accola in all the world!

"About that stuff they been yelling—" the corporal didn't look at Bullard—"that you really ate— Hey!"

Cannibal Bullard was headed for the flank, making infantrymen jump for their lives as the pony bore down.

"What the hell! Hey!" the corporal yelled.

Bullard's pony sliced between two wagons. It knocked over a stack of rifles and kicked dirt on a group of cavalrymen sitting in a circle. The cursed like troopers, which they were.

Then the corporal got started. The captain who had stopped the pair a few moments before was already after Bullard, and was yelling for support as he went.

Even with bullets snarling past him, Cannibal Bullard felt better than he had at any time since leaving the squaws' camp. Pursuit was hot, but he had made no mistake when he picked the pony. He rode well, and he held his big body low. He reached the trees with only a trifling bullet gash in his broad hind parts. His strung-out pursuers were still coming when a bugle signaled them back.

"What the hell was we after him for?" a trooper asked a companion, who shrugged and asked someone else.

In the end they all looked at the captain. He glared and was silent, trying hard to convey the impression that the matter was too weighty and confidential to be discussed.

Cannibal Bullard stopped his pony in the trees. His big laugh rang out. To hell with white men, especially those in the Army. All they ever had tried to do was kill him. He hadn't said anything about the guns. No harm was done. Why, he could tell Iron Buffalo he had gone to the Army to see if they had any cannons hidden in the wagons or ambulances. The damned cold-faced Iron Buffalo wouldn't believe that, but still he could have no bellyache about the other guns.

The whole thing had been Iron Buffalo's fault—him

and that blab-mouthed Lieutenant Accola. Colonel, he was now . . .

Bullard began to rehearse his lie. Better do it with lots of boasting about how he'd ridden through a whole United States Army.

The blue mass began to move as Bullard watched. It went at the infantry's pace toward a green valley between two purple mesas. No individual in it could guess why a wild, bearded man had ridden in chased by Indians, then scooted away even faster than he'd come.

Even if he had known that Cannibal Bullard once had been an artillery sergeant, Colonel Accola wouldn't have had the least idea why the man had fled so abruptly, for Accola had never testified at a court-martial in all his life.

Old Stub's black campaign hat was dusty and sweat-stained. He had no stars on his shoulder. His uniform was the same he had worn last night. From a distance the general was an untidy, indifferent horseman among well-dressed aides. At close range the boring thrust of his dark eyes, the way he held and turned his head told who commanded.

He was envious as he thought of the signals they had seen that morning, heliograph flashes on the mountains, executed in rapid and workmanlike manner. So far, all the Army knew about the Indians was that ten of them had chased a white man almost to the advance party. Then the white man, generally reported to have looked like a lunatic, had streaked for timber while being escorted to Colonel Accola. Old Stub thought sourly that what the Indians probably knew about the Army included the cut of Lieutenant Collins' mustache and the number of footsore infantry riding the supply wagons. Someday the bombproof gentlemen would pay more attention to communications. Maybe that surgeon who had the idea about waving flags was on the right track.

Old Stub put his glasses on the green valley ahead. It was about a half mile wide and a mile long. Steep sides, perhaps a hundred feet high, led from the valley floor to flanking mesas. About midway of the length of the valley the slopes were carved with several wide gullies. Run a crossbar between the gullies on both sides, consider the mesas as wide legs and you had a large capital H. Old Stub studied the gullies. They appeared wide enough for men to ride four abreast. He looked above the mesas, where ridge after ridge of aspen thickets rose, punctured by rock formations that thrust up like gray islands above a green sea. Hellish country to fight in back there, worse than the trees and rocks below Little Roundtop.

Old Stub had given orders that parties of less than twenty were not to explore the trees. All the way from Camp Pike no less than three companies on each flank had beaten the thickets. They might be getting a little careless by now, the general thought. It would be well to give those woods on both sides of the valley ahead a thorough shaking down.

He spoke, and Lieutenant Collins wrote.

Presently one eyebrow went up in General Montell's broad forehead. The dispatch in his hand read: *Have flanking companies penetrate no less than one half mile into trees on both sides of valley ahead.*

Montell glared at an aide. "Why doesn't his bully boy Gross do some of the dirty work? I've already had four horses injured in this confounded thicket prowling!"

Unaware of the contents of the dispatch, the aide said nothing. He wrote when Montell dictated.

Presently Old Stub saw couriers galloping to overhaul

both flanking parties. He noted the fact automatically. What he couldn't have known was that the couriers carried messages that read: *Scout edges of thickets only. Keep bulk of men from sight. I want no more injured mounts.*

General Montell really did love horses. He'd been known to weep over stories of wounded horses in Civil War actions. He thrilled to tales of gallant animals that went on, holding their places in the line after their riders had been shot from the saddle.

To Armand Montell the charge of the 15th English Hussars at Villers-en-Couche was all the military history he needed to know. One of Montell's ancestors had been in that battle. Though the ancestor had been one of the ten thousand French who ran from the three hundred and twenty-nine English cavalry, that small item in no way affected Montell's great admiration for the charge.

"Ruin my horses' legs and bellies in his damned tangled thickets!" Montell muttered.

Things were going too well to suit Old Stub. He felt the way he had at Chancellorsville just before Stuart's cavalry pried into that weak spot on the Union right flank and screened the way for Jackson's corps to walk in uninvited.

Let them think he was an old woman. If some of them had their way they'd be splitting the army into platoons, riding here and there in an effort to surround Indians from seven different directions. Maybe the Indians had slipped back to the plains to gobble up more supply trains. Maybe they weren't here at all. In private the hunches of the two scouts had sounded convincing. Before the staff the two had stumbled and looked silly, with every one of their words another bayonet thrust at their own ideas. Old Stub regretted exposing the scouts like that.

He realized that some of their resentment over the way they had been ridiculed had recoiled against him. When he'd had them listen to Corporal Thompson's full report of Indians encountered and country covered in his ride from Freeland, Babcock and Phillips had asked no questions of the courier and had informed Old Stub only when asked for information.

The courier from Freeland had reported no large bodies of Indians. That could be. It wouldn't take many to pick off a few couriers each day.

Before the Army left the mountains Old Stub vowed that he would know whether there was any substance to the rumored Indian union. If there was a camp, or had been a camp of any magnitude, he'd find out about it. But it would be the sure, slow way, not any hell-for-leather riding deal that might get hundreds of men killed unnecessarily.

The Army moved on.

Old Stub studied the country ahead once more. He saw the flanking parties disappear once more into the trees. Far ahead on the mesas he saw two scouts riding each side. The advance detail was midway through the green valley. It was a warm day. Sunlight glinted on strings of beaver ponds all the way through the left side of the valley.

Some infantry companies near the wagons were booming out *John Brown's Body*. Two horses in the herd reared high, pawing backs ahead of them and neighing. Then they settled down to the level of the rest of the dusty animals. A mule pulling a blacksmith's forge and limber snaked its gray head sidewise to bite at a black horse edging too close from the pressure of the herd.

Wagons stirring dust, ambulances looking like small prairie schooners, cavalry and walking men—the Army moved closer to the green valley.

Lieutenant Collins coughed from dust, and then stroked both wings of his yellow mustache to see whether they had been seriously disarranged by the jar.

It was, Old Stub thought, a good army. They should have had more late Civil War issue of rifles and carbines; there was a lot of green stuff in the infantry, though the lumps were leavened by wide distribution of regulars; the engineers didn't have all the tools they needed for building mountain roads; some of the high officers were not of Old Stub's choosing; and there was no artillery.

But it was a pretty good army, Old Stub thought.

With just his head showing above a rock, Iron Buffalo stood on a granite hill overlooking aspen thickets, a narrow, bare mesa and a green valley receiving blue columns. Naked to the waist, bronze and slender, he stood with arms folded on his scarred chest. There was no feather in his dark-brown hair, no war paint on his face or body. The puckered scars on his back moved a little as he breathed. None of those behind him could guess that most of his weight was on his good leg.

Looking at the scarred back where rawhide thongs had pulled through the flesh to free the weight of dragging buffalo skulls, deep-chested Bad Jaw reflected that many had done the Sun Dance. Iron Buffalo was a warrior, it was true, with many coups and brave things done. It was strange that Iron Buffalo more often than not did not care to take the scalps that were his.

There were other warriors, some much younger than Iron Buffalo, who had taken many scalps and done as many or more brave things than Iron Buffalo. Yet from none of them came the feeling of the spirit of the sky, a feeling of great power—the things that came to a man sometimes in his dream after the purification, the sweating and the fasting. In Iron Buffalo one saw these things and felt them. He breathed these feelings with his words; they came from his solemn eyes. Holy things had happened to him. Even strange Indians from far lands, even ancient enemies of the Teton saw and knew that such was true.

It would be best, Bad Jaw thought, if Iron Buffalo sat high in the rocks with the old chiefs and made the sun talk; but that could not be. He must be in the fighting. Rolled tight and tied in the mane of one of Iron Buffalo's ponies Bad Jaw had seen the old war bonnet She Who Rides had made long ago. It was old. Some of the feathers were stained, some were broken. But Iron Buffalo would not let She Who Rides make the war bonnet new again.

Though warriors would follow their own chiefs, which was good and had to be, it was Iron Buffalo in the old war bonnet that everyone would ask about when there was a moment's rest from fighting. If Iron Buffalo was killed or wounded, bad medicine would be on the fighting for all.

Without limping the slender chief walked from the hill. Around him were more warriors than trees. And so it was in the thickets far beyond sight and in the trees across the valley. If the blue soldiers who ride far wide of the army came through the trees, the fighting would start sooner than the Indians wanted. But that could not be helped.

Iron Buffalo had been afraid last night that those who had fought much in the other places would be too full of victory to gather for the big army; but they had come soon after the sun was straight above, and without being seen by the army they had gone to the places where their chiefs said.

To get here for the big fighting the warriors had let many circles of the riding soldiers get away. The way those soldiers had fought from the rocks it had not been hard for the chiefs and *akicita* members to bring the young men away. The blue coats had gone down the valley, carrying their wounded with them, catching loose horses as they went; and still they had been full of much fight.

"We should watch the old ones and their sun talk," Iron Buffalo said. He had said that so many times that those who heard were tired of hearing, but they would watch.

"We are ready here," Bad Jaw said.

"Those here have nothing but the waiting left," Iron Buffalo agreed. "Let us ride hidden by the trees and hills to where the others are gathering behind the blue army. Some of the young men may grow bold and be seen too soon."

Bad Jaw started up the hill.

Iron Buffalo followed without limping. He was glad his pony was not far away.

Billy Munro tried not to hobble as he went along beside Dan Beavers. His feet were as sore as they would ever get if he lived to be a thousand. His left sock—that damned left sock!—had worked down and bunched around his heel again. He had pulled it loose when they stopped to eat at noon, but there it was again, all hot and damp, with the back of his tendons rasping against wrinkled, dry leather. Those big shoes left over from some giant of the Civil War had been fine in camp, but now after almost four days of tramping they were showing their true character.

Beavers watched Munro's uneven gait for a while. "You should have taken the sock off, Billy, and wore nothing but axle grease on that foot."

Munro didn't answer. He was beginning to believe Johannes and Beavers had been telling the truth when they suggested that. He had tried to keep the sock up by tying a piece of strap from his knapsack around his ankle, but that hadn't worked. Maybe he'd try the axle grease the next time they stopped. The trouble with the Army, Munro decided, fully convinced that he had made a wonderful and original discovery—was that the damned shoes didn't fit.

He walked without limping when he saw Sergeant Mullins watching him again. Pretty soon old Hairy Ears would want him to ride on a wagon, with all the others making fun and asking him if things in Ohio had been different. Billy Munro vowed he'd walk just as far as the next man, even Dan Beavers.

"Where's all your Indians, Dan?" Billy asked.

Beavers grinned. "By now they're back on the plains scalping each other and capturing supply trains bringing bullets for guns we don't have."

The first cavalry units of the main body began to enter the green valley. It was nearing four o'clock.

Rafe Winburn had been lying on his back long enough for the front of him to start drying. Mica flakes gleamed like sprinkled silver in the mud cakes plastering him.

He'd dried and cleaned his pistol, oiling it from the little lead bottle in his shirt pocket. With the weapon resting on his chest he pressed his wounded calf a little deeper into the cold mud. He looked at the sky through tall green grass, watching a ladybug crawling on a blade.

It was only half-past noon. He dozed a little and waited.

Pounding hoofs brought his eyes wide open. Careful not to make a violent disturbance in the grass, he got on his side and raised his head to see two blue riders coming fast on the broad trail of the Army. He lay quite still until he was sure of saddles, boots, color of faces and short hair.

Then he rose and yelled.

Minutes later he was behind the saddle with a trooper whose face was much lighter than it had been a short time before. The couriers were from one of the relay stations Old Stub had strung out on his back trail. So far they had come only seven miles. The army was ten miles ahead at least, Winburn estimated.

"Jesus Christ!" the man ahead of Winburn said for the fourth time since hearing Winburn's story. Both messengers turned worried eyes on the rolling grasslands ahead, on the tree-clad hills at the sides.

"We'll make it all right," the second courier said.

They pressed their horses just a little harder.

Brothers they were, Winburn had noted. Maybe twins. Young, clean-faced and full of life, as he had been thirty-five years before. His tale had scared them, but they were going ahead to carry him and his news and their own dispatches from Colonel Nelson at Camp Pike, saying that the Power in Denver had at last agreed to let the army have six howitzers—if Old Stub would send a detail after them.

Winburn's leg began to ache. He was stiff and sore from his long walk and the lying in icy mud and water for many hours.

He looked a trifle enviously at the youth and spring of the two brothers. Well, a man couldn't do like the fellow in the Bible did with the sun. . . .

The end of the narrow mesa Babcock and Geore Phillips were approaching sloped gently to rising parklands on ahead, open country that was being crowded harder and harder by mountains on both sides. Behind them came three companies of cavalry, crashing their horses a short distance into the edge of the aspens.

Across a green valley on the scouts' right they saw two other civilian riders nearing the end of a mesa. Now and then they saw the flash of blue uniforms in the trees behind the other pair of scouts. Gross's four brigades of cavalry were more than halfway through the green valley; infantry battalions were in the middle of the cross-bar of the H; the baggage train was just inside the lower end of the valley; the horse herd was at the entrance; and Montell's two cavalry brigades was half a mile behind.

"You know," Babcock said, "in a way it ain't a bad idee to eat meals at certain times like we been doing."

"It's all right," Phillips said. "But it gets tiresome knowing you're going to do things at a certain time. It's like the fellow—"

He stiffened upward in the saddle as one trying to ease an aching back. Echoes from a shot that had come from the thicket to the left rolled across the green valley.

Babcock shot twice with his Spencer. "How bad, G'ore?"

They were moving into a gallop. Phillips was hunched forward, his left elbow pressing his side, his hands clenched. "I can ride," he said.

Among the trees on the hill to their left a Modoc chief looked angrily at a young warrior lying behind a log. "No sun signals!" the chief said.

But when they looked across the valley an instant later light was flashing from four high places on the rock hills.

Looking past Phillips, Babcock saw ponies coming from thickets on both sides of the plain, far ahead of the advance party. On the opposite mesa the two scouts were racing ahead. Babcock looked behind him.

A few troopers from the three companies in the edge of the trees had come out on the narrow flat. They were galloping hard along the mesa, watching the thickets, their carbines free of scabbards.

"All right, G'ore?" Babcock yelled.

Phillips didn't answer. He suddenly slipped from his saddle, sprawling and rolling loosely on the ground.

Babcock heard the thickets behind him explode. A few balls were whispering past him when he leaped from his horse. Reins in one hand, he knelt beside Phillips and saw the soak of blood just above the wounded man's left hip. As he lifted Phillips from the ground, Babcock noted grimly that he'd never heard such rocking crashing of rifle fire as were coming from the trees. Yet the little firing there had been from the aspens immediately on his left had stopped.

Babcock's horse almost got away when he draped his partner across the saddle.

Where rocks rose above the trees, a kneeling group of Minneconjous watched the scouts, holding their fire. "The tall one has a strong heart to save his brother," a young warrior said.

Eyes grim above his wide cheekbones, a dark chief

in war bonnet raised his Springfield. "We fight today like the white man," he said angrily.

He shot.

Babcock's horse humped and leaped. Phillips slid from the saddle, and the animal plunged away.

The chief reached into his breechclout for another cartridge.

Babcock picked up his partner's body and ran for the edge of the mesa. One bullet and a few clear whoops followed him. He went over the side and ran at an angle down the slope. Phillips was dead, he knew. The same bullet that hit the horse had first entered the back of the scout's head. The three pits that had formed a triangle over Phillips' left eye were gone now.

Babcock kept going toward the beaver ponds below. Before steep rock sides slowed him down he heard the thump of light cannons at his back.

From where old Fighting Bear sat, hunched on a rock in the thickets above the right leg of the H, a gilt-framed mirror on his lap, one could see most of the valley and the two mesas.

The advance party had recoiled toward the upper end of the valley. They had dismounted in a line, watching the Indian cavalry forming half a mile or more beyond. Only a few ponies were coming from the thickets now. There were not more than five hundred Indians in the open ahead of the advance detail. But still waiting in the trees were three times that number, Blackfeet, Buffalo Cree, half of the Ojibway, Boise and Bruneau Shoshoni, Malheurs and some Tonto Apaches. There were others, too, that Fighting Bear could not remember, but he knew they were there, waiting to see if the soldiers would chase the few far enough so that the many could cut between the blue-coats and the army.

All the cavalry brigades at the head of the blue army were moving on at a trot. They were shifting formations, but it was hard to tell what they were about to do.

Walking soldiers in the middle of the valley were halted, and so were the horse herds and the baggage train. The rear detail was coming in fast. Montell's two brigades were moving closer to the mouth of the valley. Across on the wide left H-leg, the three companies who had been riding flank had burst from the trees and were trying to reach the edge of the mesa.

Order was lost among them. Horses were falling, and men were rolling or crawling on the ground. Some were running on foot to get over the edge of the mesa. Smoke was beginning to rise above the trees, and rifle fire seemed to be even heavier.

Messengers were scurrying to and from Old Stub near the infantry regiments. There were flurries of riders around brigade standards up and down the valley.

Fighting Bear saw all of this, interpreting it in his own way as far as any meaning could be gathered from the lack of general movement. It was too much to see at once, the old Brule thought.

Most of all, he was interested in seeing that the one scout on the opposite mesa had carried the other from the hill and was nearing the beaver ponds below.

It was a brave thing to do, Fighting Bear thought.

Just then the cannon fire began.

Most of the canister fell among the infantry. The shells were not large, and they came irregularly but fast from the hills above the left H-leg. Each burst sent two and a half dozen one-ounce balls snarling among the infantry, digging at legs, stomachs, arms, eyes—wherever a thousand factors sent the lead.

A few shells screamed out to burst among the brigades of cavalry trotting up the valley.

But it was the infantry that took the beating.

Sweating faces yelled. Arms waved signals. Noncoms cursed. The infantry went into a left flank movement that was ragged and unco-ordinated at first. Then order came. On the double, the columns moved toward the hill. Bugles sounded from the front regiments of cavalry, and some of them went toward the hill on their left. Some went straight ahead. A brigade cut to the right, going toward the top of the right H-leg.

Canister still burst as the blue masses moved. Infantrymen fell. Horses with lead in their bellies screamed and bolted.

As statistics of such things go, the army was not hurt. Those blue men lying still or twisting on the trampled green grass were but a small fraction of the total force. The army had been stung a little; that was all. To those who writhed or crawled, or got on hands and knees with backs humped, that last fact would have been difficult to explain. To many lying still it didn't matter.

For all its largeness, the blue mass preserved good order as it crowded the beaver dams under the protecting rise of the mesa. Canister was still whizzing from where shells tore turf in the middle of the valley.

Mirrors winked and the guns stopped.

The army got ready to fight back.

Ahead of the advance party, the line of Indians began to ride. They came in as though they intended to cleave clear down the valley. Lieutenants shouted. Sergeants bellowed. Most of those who were nervously raising Springfield or Sharps carbines lowered them. Some of those facing their first Indian charge took time to look right and left, trying to size up their own strength against what looked like ten thousand savages almost on top of them.

Short and heavy in his saddle, a ruddy major with a bushy gray goatee rode slowly past the front of the dismounted troopers.

"Hold your fire, men. Wait for orders." He smiled. "We'll shoot them they get in range—if they ever do. Hold your fire . . ."

His smile and words were steadying. But men leaned sideways to see around his horse, as though fearful that the awful horde would cover half a mile and be among them while the major's horse was still obstructing vision.

Dust rolling behind the charging Indians suddenly seemed to catch up and envelope them. Some of the troopers had seen the mirror flashes that sprang from the hands of chiefs riding in front of the line. Out of the dust smoke came flashes of lean bodies leaping to the ground. Most of the Indians knelt. White puffs blossomed in the dust smoke.

No one among the soldiers gave an order to fire, but carbine butts went against blue wool. Horse holders held tight to jerking leather when the crashes came.

Five or six troopers staggered or fell.

"By God!" the major cried. "They're outranging us!" His quick order to lie down was not necessary.

The major still sat his horse, his thoughts bitter as he saw increasing evidence among the horses that the savages out ahead were shooting better arms than United States troops. The major was a cavalryman at heart, but he was no fool. He had fought Indians before the war, when he'd been a brand-new lieutenant. He knew they probably wouldn't stand a massed charge, but before they turned and ran they would leave a good many empty saddles.

He put his glasses on the trees to the right and left beyond the Indians in sight. He saw nothing but trees and rock hills. But the major was not a fool.

He ordered the horse holders to move back and told his men to hold.

A courier was streaking toward the advance detail from the main body. One of Gross's regiments was coming straight ahead. On each flank a brigade was bending out, one headed toward the sloping end of the mesa at the top of the right H-leg, the other going left.

Once clear of the brigades on its flanks the regiment coming straight on hinged out into a massed line. Trumpeters extended themselves.

A captain beside the major spoke. "Wide intervals, sir, to let them through?"

The major didn't hesitate. "Wide intervals, hell! That's Matthews' regiment. We'll see what he has in mind. Maybe I'll have to lecture a little on Indian tactics."

Red and yellow pennons flapping a little in the still air, the regiment came on at a trot. The major's horse shot down to meet Colonel Matthews. When the blue troopers galloped up the narrowing park in a charge a few minutes later, they were in three bodies. The left flank was composed of the advance detail. Like the other flanking body, the advance party was headed for the trees. The center could take care of the Indians straight ahead.

And the center did. When they crossed the ground from which the dismounted Indians had been firing, there were no Indians lying on the ground, though troopers had seen them fall. There were empty saddles in the blue line, more than Colonel Matthews had expected.

Just out of range of carbine fire were bobbing rumps

of ponies, carrying riders who looked back now and then to yell. Colonel Matthews had listened intelligently to the major from the advance detail, but now he lost his head and led the charge to overtake the ponies.

Officers and troopers not too engrossed in their efforts to get at the will-o'-the-wisps ahead heard a sudden renewal of artillery fire.

It sounded much louder than before.

On the mesa that formed the wide right leg of the H, Captain Edwin Axford, once a justice of the peace in Urbana, Illinois, a private in the 16th Ohio Cavalry the second year of the war, held his gray horse steady while he leveled binoculars on the largest puffs of smoke above the trees beyond the mesa, across the valley.

All of the three companies had come from the trees behind him. Two lieutenants set their horses beside Axford.

Someone at those hidden batteries—probably a white man, Axford thought—had sense enough to elevate the guns high in an effort to lob shells on the Army under the protecting drop of the mesa side. Most of the light shells burst out in the valley, but now and then one dropped where it hurt. Axford saw one explosion among cavalry swimming their horses across a big beaver dam at the bottom of the wide gullies.

He saw Gross's brigades, two bright streams of blue racing for the top ends of the H to strike the Indian flanks. Flanks? Axford asked himself. So far there had been no firing from the thickets above the north mesa, on which he now was. He felt a sense of guilt about those trees at his back. He should have ignored Montell's order and gone high on the hills, instead of lurking just out of sight in the aspens. He wondered how deep the three companies across from him had gone. They had suffered terribly from the opening fire, not many of them reaching safety over the mesa edge.

He gave his orders.

The three companies dismounted. They deployed in skirmish order and started for the trees.

It was then the rock points above the trees seemed to come apart from artillery fire. Every tree turned into a rifle. Smoke drifted sinuously above the trembling aspens. A third of the three companies went down in the first burst. Those who could turned and ran for the edge of the mesa. Many of them died or fell on the way. Bullets chopped into the horse holders, striking their charges with the solid, sodden impact of lead against flesh. Most of the mounts ran wild.

No one carried wounded.

The mesa was approximately a hundred yards wide. Not far for a man to run ordinarily, but a brutally long distance when he is a target. All the way to the edge rifle fire left blue bundles on the purple flat. Less than thirty men went over the edge of the hill.

Captain Axford was with them. On his right hand, tendons showed dirty gray at the edge of a hole where the two middle knuckles had been. Bright blood was spurting from the hand.

Above the survivors shells made *tzuuming* sounds as they slanted toward the center of the Army across the valley.

Still, statistics would have shown that the Army had not suffered greatly. But, when projectiles from the newly active artillery began to strike, even statistics changed.

Captain Axford ripped his neckerchief off. He held it in his teeth and pressed his right wrist with strong fingers. "Martin—" he waited until the trooper lying flat twisted toward him—"cut off what's left of these two fingers."

A little later, neckerchief pressed against his wound, Axford took inventory. He was the only officer left. He sent five of his twenty-eight men down the hill to seek shelter and wait for medical aid.

Not a rifle was firing in the thickets above them now. The artillery was working hard.

"Up to the rim of the hill!" Axford ordered. "Fire into the smoke around those cannons!"

At his headquarters beside a beaver pond, Old Stub went over the situation quickly in his mind. His short gray beard framed by the open points of his coat collar, he was sitting straighter in his saddle than he ordinarily did. Old Stub was far more worried about the right flank than the one on the left. He'd stopped the cavalry from floundering in the beaver ponds. They were dismounted now and going across like the infantry. Men were scaling the rocks, and some were concentrating in the gullies. Noncoms and officers were working well. Before long he'd have a regiment of infantry and a regiment of dismounted cavalry in position under the rim of the mesa.

As soon as Gross's Second Brigade got in flanking position at the top of the left H-leg, and the brigade Montell had sent from the rear, Hickaman's, got in place at the bottom of the left H-leg, the attack would start.

Gross had sent his Fourth Brigade to flank the trees at the top of the right H-leg. That was good. If those hills on that side stayed silent, the brigade would be in a position to sweep down into the upper end of the valley in case a large-scale cavalry threat developed from straight ahead.

Surgeons were getting their headquarters set up. Details were bringing in wounded from the middle of the valley.

Still Old Stub was worried about the silent hills on the right flank. It wasn't like Indians to use only one jaw of a trap.

He began to dictate dispatches to Lieutenant Collins, whose hand didn't falter or tremble as he wrote. There was a pretty cool brain behind those awful yellow mustaches, Old Stub thought.

Couriers left the general's headquarters with orders for Montell to send a regiment to flank the hills from the bottom of the right H-leg; with a dispatch ordering the quartermaster in charge of the wagons to form them across the mouth of the valley for defense, leaving intervals for cavalry sorties. He sent orders to Gross to send a regiment of cavalry to the gullies where the crossbar of the H intersected the right leg. Old Stub sent a battalion of infantry toward the same place.

The infantrymen went on the double, files spread wide to maintain damage from the light artillery at their backs.

Old Stub's dark eyes bored at the silent hills on the right. He saw the three companies on the mesa dismount, deploy and near the thickets.

An instant later he saw the skirmish line wither. Shrapnel screamed across the valley to cut and gouge and kill with hot, twisting steel splinters. A bulge showed in the middle of one of the cavalry columns crossing the valley. Blue men and horses lay scattered on the ground. Another shell tore a gap in a file of infantry.

Officers ordered the reserve battalion of infantry near Old Stub to lie down at the edge of the beaver ponds. Some huddled against the face of the dams. One company went shoulder-deep in a pond when they stepped beyond a narrow underwater ledge. Forage caps floated on the water. Brown faces gasped convulsively at the hard shock of icy water.

Ten men crossing between dams to join the attack on the south mesa were drowned when a shell broke a big dam. The quick surge of water took out the next dam below and drowned more men.

Shrapnel sent its flying, twisted steel fingers among men climbing the steep sides of the mesa, among men concentrated in the gullies.

Canister was coming, too, from both sides. As soon as soldiers left the protecting lee of the left hill and started across the valley, light artillery had opened once more from the hills above the left H-leg.

It was too late to withdraw from the valley. Old Stub's face went bleak and grim. The attacks would have to go ahead. Besides, the artillery couldn't fire forever. He did not leave his horse.

Some of the soldiers struggling in the edges of the beaver ponds thought the guns had already been firing forever. Those who had to cross the valley were sure of it. But still they went on to strike that mesa above the right H-leg.

The heavier guns from the north stopped first. Not because they lacked targets, but because a tremendous black-bearded white man with bulging, staring eyes was making his big voice heard.

"They got to cool off! To cool off!" Bellowing like a demon he raced from one rock hill to another.

A Piegan brave carrying sponging water in a leather

bucket from a spring at the base of one of the rock hills got the idea quickly. He threw the icy water on the barrel of a smoking six-pound Wiard steel cannon. That made one gun less above the north mesa.

There was one less warrior, too, for Cannibal Bullard knocked the Indian off a rock ledge and broke his back.

One less Indian didn't matter.

There were still plenty on the north hills—nearly four thousand of them, which was not quite as many as were on the hills above the south mesa across the valley.

Over there, above the left leg of the H, the guns had cooled because the gunners, mainly Nez Percé and Navajo, for sometime had seen no large, close masses of blue the two-pounders would reach easily. For a while they had shot high, trying to lob shells on the soldiers near the beaver dams. Though mirror flashes from across the valley had said they were doing fairly well, the gunners had been unable to see their shells land. To most of them the burst was what counted. So, not being able to observe their own handiwork, the gunners forgot the soldiers by the river and dropped occasional shells on the blue men across the valley.

Then chiefs made their voices heard. All the south guns were silent. Remembering well Bullard's profane instructions, the chiefs had warriors run up the screws to depress muzzles for covering the south mesa.

Indians on both sides of the valley shifted a little to get better rifle bearing on the narrow strips of purple flats the blue men would have to cross.

Though the figures would never be known, except as an indistinguishable part of a cold total, so far the Army had 3,100 casualties, 1,800 of whom were dead. Individual units losing the highest percentage of men were the six outriding companies of cavalry, which had followed expressly Montell's orders not to get far enough into the trees and rocks to injure horses.

The Indians had fourteen dead and twenty-seven wounded, all but four of the casualties having been inflicted by Gross's regiment, which had chased the Indians in the park above the upper end of the valley. The Indians' casualties were rather high, considering that they had been fighting from cover, supported by artillery, or scampering away from pursuers whose carbines didn't carry quite far enough.

Captain Axford's twenty-odd survivors had done very well, though they didn't know it. By lying under the mesa rim and firing at the yellowish billows of smoke from the rock hills, they had wounded four gunners.

Looking at the men coming up the hill behind him, Axford cursed when he saw that some of the cavalry apparently intended to ride up the wide gullies. He scrambled down the hill and told a captain at the head of a mounted group: "There's holes by the hundreds at the top of these gullies! They're about a foot deep—been covered with twigs and grass!"

The captain listened. He dismounted his troops and sent messengers to warn those still on their horses in the other gullies. After being stopped by officers who thought they were running away, ducking occasional canister and having trouble breaking through columns, the couriers began to pass the word.

One captain said: "Holes, huh? We got orders to get those guns. My command will dismount after we cross that little flat up there."

A lieutenant wanted to know what kind of holes.

Not having seen them the messenger said: "Holes. Hell's sake! Just holes, I guess."

The lieutenant yelled at his men: "Look out for holes

when we reach the top!" He thought he'd feel better riding across the mesa than on foot. His men, he was sure, must feel the same.

Another lieutenant told a courier: "We'll jump any damn holes they got!" He wished he could be out in the open, riding straight at the sneaking red devils, instead of being jammed in a damned gulch.

The fourth courier found a major. "Sir, there's holes —" and then a one-ounce canister ball tore one cheekbone away. The messenger sat down on a rock, shaking his head, his eyes wide-open and blank.

"Go to the rear!" the major ordered.

In spite of the confusion of men lost from their companies, of conflicting shouts and orders, the attack began to form.

Infantry spread out under the mesa rim and began to shoot into the trees. Some shot blindly. Old hands aimed at the rock points above the aspens. They got some of the gunners around the silent pieces and forced old Fighting Bear to slide down behind a granite slab. He held carefully to his gilt-framed mirror.

When sun signals came from the rocks across the valley to tell that the assault was about to start on the north hills, Fighting Bear tilted his glass to catch the sun. Other mirrors talked. Indian watchers saw the flashes above the rising wisps of smoke and warned other Indians to get ready.

Cannibal Bullard began to bellow. He was beside a twelve-pounder, a three-inch cannon that could hurl a fourteen-pound projectile nearly three miles. Its sliding wedge breech operated from a side lever, and even a damned Indian could understand it worked just like a rifle as far as loading.

There were three other twelve-pounders in the battery. On the rock knobs close by were two more batteries of two-pounders. Bullard himself had tipped the Wiard off its rock ledge and down on the Piegan who had ruined it. It lay across the Indian's broken legs. From the points of contact with flesh, nauseating smoke was curling. The Piegan's eyes were open. He was alive.

Cannibal Bullard had cause to bellow. The guns had been well placed for shooting into the valley, but they could not be depressed enough to sweep the mesa below him.

He had to be content with killing blue men clinging to the hill across the valley when he shouted for the guns to open fire.

Clouds of yellowish smoke began to rise again. The rock hills trembled.

Men across the valley began to die. Others cursed their comrades on the north side for not getting up to cross that mesa, plunge into the trees and stop those guns and whirring fragments.

Officers below the rim of the north mesa, the wide right leg of H, wondered where their flanking support was. They had no way of knowing that it was almost in place at the top of the H-leg, and coming up fast after a late start toward the bottom of the right leg.

From the valley Old Stub could see where the flanking support was. He had given orders for the center to hold its frontal attack until the wings were engaged. Now all he could do was watch and wait.

When rifle fire began to build up heavy all at once, in the thickets above the north mesa, several officers under the rim misconstrued it as meaning that the flanks were starting their drive. The sudden flurry of small arms shooting meant no more than that the Indians in the trees had caught a fever to hit all the heads and arms and tiny movements that showed behind the smoke of soldiers firing over the rim of the mesa.

Then most of Bullard's light artillery stopped to cool.

The blue men on the north hill went up and over.

Mounted cavalrymen ran into trouble right away. Dozens of the foremost horses went down when their legs went into a clever pattern of evil little holes that had been dug to fit shod hooves snugly. Horses piled up. The way was blocked. It took time to dismount men who should have been dismounted ten minutes before.

Unimpeded by the little traps, dismounted cavalrymen and infantry went forward and took the beating from an awful fire that almost obscured the thickets.

The captain who had sent messengers to warn about the holes took his men up dismounted. Therefore they reached the mesa without difficulty and were killed sooner.

The lieutenant who had said his men would jump "any damn holes they got!" actually did ride across the trap. Some of his men followed. They went straight into the trees, presumably to saber gunners. So far into the thickets did the lieutenant ride before he fell that the Indians considered him a brave man. Many rose to strike his body. Afterward, he was cited for bravery. Twenty years later his family received a medal. No one knew that he had earned another distinction—that of being the first man scalped in the battle that later became known as Green Valley.

Indian riflemen ripped the turf with such a terrible volume of fire that not more than four hundred soldiers reached the edge of the trees. They flung themselves flat and began to fire ahead. They fired steadily into the smoke until their ammunition began to run low. Even then the Indians didn't care to come off the hills and go knee to knee with them. Not that the Indians were afraid, but they had good cover where they were.

And they had checked the attack.

Soldiers who had made the edges of the thicket lay there, unable to go ahead or retreat.

Those who had returned to the shelter of the hillside did not want to try that open space again—not right away, at least. Even their officers didn't blame them.

Some cursed. A few prayed silently. Everybody waited for the flanking cavalry to start its action.

Horses with broken legs or pulled tendons hobbled in the open. Others ran wildly to get away from this man-made hell, some plunging straight into the smoke and rags of flame coming from the trees. A big sorrel with a bullet in its hind quarters screamed shrilly, pawing with its forefeet in an effort to rise. The calks of its shoes were tearing the clothes from an infantryman who lay with a broken leg and a bullet-shattered arm. He kept crying hoarsely: "Won't *somebody* help me!"

A cavalryman whose pale blond hair spilled over a bleeding forehead as he crawled finally dragged the wounded man back. His pleas never changed. They only grew weaker as he bled to death.

Exultant war whoops came from the smoke-shrouded trees. Troopers lying at the base of the hill beyond the mesa could hear the bellows of a white man who shouted Indian talk and cursed in English. They cursed and tried to pick him off by sound.

Indians killed loose horses, sent lead at huddled bundles of blue clothing when they stirred. Horses crashed down on the wounded and dead. A trooper who showed no visible wound suddenly stood up in the middle of the mesa. He walked in a circle until his body jerked from striking bullets and he fell clawing at the earth.

A trooper whose red hair gleamed in the smoke crawled toward the mesa rim. The sharp point of a broken leg bone stuck through the flesh and dug a little furrow as he dragged himself.

"No!" he said as he saw an infantryman coming out to help him. "No! Stay back!"

The wounded man's face dissolved in a welter of blood. The infantryman, who had not stopped, rolled on his side and tried with dusty fingers to push back ropes of entrails spilling through his ripped tunic.

From the rocks and trees the barbaric shouting was louder and more chilling than Rebel yells of early in the war.

For the time, at least, this assault across the wide right leg of the H was stopped. It would start again. It had to move again, or else shrapnel would chew up everybody by the beaver ponds and on the hill across the valley.

In the trees a mile down the brown grasslands at the rear of the army, Iron Buffalo put on his stained and faded war bonnet. His ragged-looking brown pony bore a vermilion lightning streak across one hip. The headdress, the zigzag mark and a strong heart were Iron Buffalo's medicine.

With far-seeing glasses he had watched the fighting. He had seen how the cannon fire drove the army to one side of the valley; he had seen the foolish soldiers who went far ahead of the army to chase decoy riders, though someone among them had been wise: part of the riders had gone to scout the trees on both sides. Iron Buffalo had watched the attack across the north mesa falter and fail.

But many blue riding soldiers had gone fast to strike at the Indians from both ends of both mesas. Iron Buffalo knew that he and all the Indians around him and all the others waiting in the thickets across the park should have started sooner to draw some of the blue men away from going to the ends of the mesas.

He turned to Bad Jaw. "Will you ride with me, my brother?"

"I will ride." Bad Jaw raised one bronze arm and shouted.

Mirrors behind him caught the sun and sent it back toward the spirit of the sky. From the trees across the wide plain came responding flashes. Four thousand cavalry that had been far back on the ridges when the army passed got ready to ride.

Only half of them, one thousand on each side of the plain, would ride at once. The other two thousand would wait to see whether they could spring the same kind of trap set for those who chased the decoys at the army's front.

From the southern thickets, led by Iron Buffalo on his zigzagged brown pony, came Brule, Unkpatila, Sans Arc, Oglala, Two Kettles and other members of the great Teton council, which was but one of the seven great councils of all the Dakotas. Fierce Minneconjous rode behind their chiefs; remnants of the Santees, who had suffered much from the white men, came eager for revenge; tall and painted rode the Cheyennes behind their great chief, Thunder Eater, while old men carried the sacred arrow bundle. There were Cayuses, some of the Modocs, half of the Ojibway, who had quarreled among themselves about following Iron Buffalo. The tall Cheyennes' brothers, wonder-riding Arapahos, brought their sacred bundle and rushed through the trees.

And still there were a thousand warriors left in the trees on the south side of the plain.

From the other side, when the sun flashed upward, came the short Comanches, the first of whom the Great Spirit had made upon a horse, so that all who came later could not walk well on the ground. Beside them were the Kiowas, a people not nearly so many as the Sioux, but killers of white men beyond counting. Kiowa Apaches came behind them, whooping as they rode. Little brown Apaches, who could fight among the rocks as well as they could ride, looked lean and deadly without the finery of their northern brothers. Crows and Snakes, Assiniboines and Sarsi shot their war-stripped ponies from the northern thickets.

But a thousand warriors on that side still held back.

In the aspens on both sides were many young boys watching the pony herd; a few of the women, and many old warriors, stayed behind to be with the canvas sacks of ammunition.

For almost three moons the warriors of all tribes had strengthened their ponies on the good grass in the long valley behind the mountains. The ponies were strong. The warriors were ready.

The two great streams of cavalry sprang from the trees and raced their ponies toward the middle of the plain. They met in the center, and even after the long run many of the young men still raced their ponies along the edges to be sure they had a good second wind.

A few of the young warriors grew excited when they saw two blue riders far down the plain. They wheeled and thundered toward them in spite of the efforts of the *akicita.*

Two hundred ponies wide, five riders deep, the Indians made two great formations. Ponies shifted against each other, some biting and kicking. Manes and feathers tossed. Like smoke dust came from the earth that had been churned by the passing of the army. Only a few lances with scalps showed above the riders. Every Indian had a rifle. Many carried short bows, too.

No sun signals flashed from the high rocks. Iron Buffalo rode along in front of the other chiefs, many thinking he should have had a better pony and a new war bonnet.

He raised both arms to the sky. In one hand was a Henry rifle.

It seemed to Bad Jaw that even the ponies seemed to understand. For a moment nothing but dust moved.

Without a cry Iron Buffalo wheeled his pony and rode toward the army.

Behind him rose a fearful shouting. Thousands of hoofs beat the brown earth. War bonnets fluttered. Dark hair streamed. The tied-up tails of Sioux ponies bobbed. Tassels of dyed horsehair and feathers danced in the tails of Coeur d'Alene ponies. Fresh scalps tied to beaded bridles lay back against the necks of Comanche war horses in full stride. Red spots rose and fell on the white croup of a Nez Percé's *appaloosa* pony.

Main bodies held good formation. Chiefs ahead rent the dust with screaming yells and tried to overtake and pass Iron Buffalo. They knew then that the ragged pony with the zigzag mark was a brother to the wind.

Iron Buffalo led the way.

It could have been the dust that fooled Montell, who had fallen back part way toward the wagons. He quit fuming at the silly way the battle was being handled when he saw the two streams of Indians charge from the thickets. Accustomed to judging cavalry numbers by familiar masses—not too well accustomed, at that—Montell told an aide that there were a good many Indians sure enough; but disorderly as they were, an inexperienced man was apt to overestimate their strength.

His final guess was one thousand.

While the Indians were riding from both sides of the park to meet each other, and during the time it took them to form, Montell considered falling back to the wagons, now placed to form a rather effective barrier across most of the lower end of the green valley. He also considered dismounting his command to fight lying down.

Finally he decided that either move would be losing dignity before a thousand painted savages who lacked the guts for a genuine stirrup-to-stirrup fight.

Major O'Meara's regiment, sent to flank the north mesa from the bottom of the right H-leg, had been late in getting started. It had taken an aide time to ride from Old Stub's headquarters with the order. Montell had taken twice as much time considering the order to send half of the brigade he had left to a place where, as any idiot could see, no action or threat of action existed.

But now Montell showed he was a decisive leader, a worthy descendant of the ancestor who had killed his horse running for Cambrai during the battle of Villers-en-Couche.

He sent an aide to recall O'Meara from flanking the hills beyond the bottom of the right H-leg. By then, of course, Montell had seen that there *was* a threat above that north mesa. He had seen the dismounted cavalry and infantry beaten back in their one assault across the purple strip. Infantry, Montell believed, was a slow, worthless mass that usually got in the way of cavalry.

There must be at least a battalion of them cringing under the rim of that mesa.

Let them get up and go do their work. Major-General Armand Montell had troubles of his own forming in the broad park at the army's rear.

He gave orders for Colonel Pritchard to form his regiment for a charge. Pritchard had never been to West Point. He had no traditions. He never had heard of Villers-en-Couche, and he didn't like Montell anyway.

After a discussion that Pritchard tried hard to keep within the bounds of reasonable protest, he grew white at Montell's references to cowardice.

"You can go to hell, General!" the colonel told Montell. "I won't take my regiment into a senseless dog fight and leave the whole damned hind end of the army exposed!"

Montell's face went as cold and gray as moonlight on bleak granite. He smiled gently without disturbing his delicate sneer.

Colonel Pritchard went toward the wagons under arrest. Major Larkins stepped into command of the regiment. It took the men a little time to form. Montell held them up until he saw his aide had reached O'Meara. As soon as O'Meara returned, his regiment—or part of it—could go down and sweep surviving Indians back into the trees where they belonged, Montell planned calmly. That is, if there were any savages still inclined to besport themselves upon the plain after Major Larkins finished with them.

After squadrons hinged out and the line massed—not quite as precisely as the general would have liked, but good enough considering that there was somewhat of an emergency—they made a sight that warmed Montell's heart.

So deeply was he stirred, he raised one hand in salute and cried: "*Audentes fortuna juvat!*"

A trooper with long eye teeth that looked like fangs sought a translation from white-faced Bonnie Dixon, since Trooper Dixon was suspected of having once studied for the ministry. "What's the old crawfish sayin'?"

Dixon looked at the two-sectioned dust storm just starting to roll. "He says the first man scalped will be commissioned."

Montell raised a delicate little sword in signal to Major Larkins.

Eight hundred and sixteen cavalrymen—including trumpeters—went straight at the dust clouds holding two thousand of the best natural cavalry this benign world ever produced. Guidons whipping, horses rocketing, dust flowing—the regiment followed its sacred orders.

"Gallant eight hundred!" Montell murmured.

An aide turned his head to look at another. He moved his lips to make two silent words: "Dirty sonofabitch!"

Just dismounting his men to filter into the trees ahead, Major O'Meara waited for the courier to reach him. "What the dirty, double-dyed hell now!" he asked.

"General Montell says return at once, sir!"

Major O'Meara looked at the plain where the dust clouds were thundering toward each other. He took a moment to cross himself, then gave orders quietly.

Montell did not know it, but he had saved the lives of many of O'Meara's men. Screened by rocks and trees on a little granite dome commanding the lower thickets, a .45-70 Gatling gun was set to look down the throats of any soldiers entering the trees.

The Indian gunners relaxed with disappointed grunts. A Cayuse warrior with gray and yellow paint streaks on his wide chest rubbed a big hand over the brass casings around the ten barrels. The shiny brass fascinated him. It had been so with a kettle of the same metal that his mother had owned when he was a little boy.

Now the casings would be cool for a while longer. He could feel and rub the shiny brass.

Still in the center, still ahead, Iron Buffalo glanced at his war rope, felt the weight of the rifle in his hand. He went straight for the soldiers coming out to meet the Indians. Maybe it was so that those behind him did not think he could be killed. Iron Buffalo did not think so himself.

"Hoka hey!" he shouted.

Bad Jaw's loud voice thundered a reply almost at Iron Buffalo's right side.

Fingers clenched in streaming manes, the warriors behind roared their war cries.

Major Larkins, now that he was in it against his better judgment, did the best he could. He split his squadrons to meet both the oncoming formations.

There on the brown plain, with the mountains high above them, the four masses met and merged.

Iron Buffalo went sidewise and down as a saber flashed. It would have severed his left arm and parted ribs to the middle of his chest. He shot a soldier in the chest. The momentum of their horses carried them past each other before the trooper fell. Iron Buffalo took another saber slash on his rifle barrel. Steel rang. The blade glanced and knocked feathers from the old war bonnet.

And then he was clear through the soldiers. He

wheeled his ragged brown pony with the lightning mark and came back.

Steel on steel. Swords carving, hacking. Shouts and groans, the screams of horses. Bitter sting of powder in eyes and nose and mouth. Dust boiling up. Distended, red-rimmed nostrils of horses looking out of the smoke. Shots and yells and shots. Teeth white in shouting faces. Blue arms killing. Naked arms killing.

A Company D trooper yelled and slashed down hard at a Quahada Comanche reloading a Springfield rifle. The Indian disappeared on the opposite side of his *grulla* pony. Only a moccasined foot showed above the pony's back. The sword severed the foot, bit deep into the horse's spine. It lunged away to fall on a wounded trooper who was kneeling with his elbows up to protect his head. Sitting in the dust with blood spurting from his ankle, the Comanche used a long knife to rip the bellies of two saddled horses before a shod hoof broke his skull.

Indians shot Indians. Troopers shot or hacked at other troops, fighting blindly against anything that ranged up in the awful dust and noise. The piercing cries of mutilated animals, quadrupeds and bipeds, rose above the dust and waved toward the clear blue sky.

This was the beautiful cavalry engagement General Montell had dreamed to see. He could see but little of it, and that little brought more gray to his cheeks.

From the time the four bodies met, the action degenerated into idiotic, frenzied killing, all leadership gone from both sides. For the blue men it became a matter of slashing or shooting to stay alive, then trying to get away. So thick was the dust, so many times had their horses wheeled, that many did not know in which direction safety lay.

His sword broken on a rifle barrel, his carbine too slow and clumsy for close quarters, Bonnie Dixon reached through the dust smoke to grab a Cheyenne by the throat. Side by side the horse and pony threshed a moment. The combatants fell struggling to the ground. Dixon rose after a while and grabbed a trailing war rope. He found the pony mean to handle, but he mounted and rode in the right direction.

A long-armed sergeant swung his carbine in a circle, yelling defiance. He clubbed a chief to death. He ducked a spinning hatchet and a war maul. A Kiowa rawhide rope snaked through the dust. Its loop fell around the sergeant's neck. Brown hands from two ponies reached out to seize the rope. They dragged the sergeant from his horse and pulled him bouncing on the trampled grass while he clutched with both hands at the noose.

There were too many Indians, too much dust and not enough blue men.

Somewhere in the hellish uproar a trumpeter still lived. He blew the order to retreat, with or without authorization no one ever knew.

The blue men went back toward the heroic general who had ordered the charge. Nearly four hundred of them started, which spoke well for the way they had fought. Ninety-eight of them managed to fight their way through the two streams of riders who had poured from the thickets between the first action of the Army.

Not all of the ninety-eight got back. Indians love a running fight. They killed all the way. They killed even when soldiers and Indians ran afoul of stampeding horses. Even in the terror of flight some of the troopers noticed that the horses were their own. Riders who looked like other soldiers were driving the herd.

Almost to the wagons the Indians pursued the remnants.

Then solid fire from behind the supply train sent the victors racing out of range.

The regiment was gone. Those who brought their wind-blown horses through the gaps between wagons numbered less than fifty.

It could be said the regiment had saved the Army by giving Major O'Meara time to come from the hill and form a tough line behind the wagons. That is the way General Montell always looked at it, easily forgetting that the dead regiment could have formed the line itself. He afterward referred to those out on the plain as "my gallant regiment that unhesitatingly flung itself against ten times its number!"

Even some of the survivors later believed what the general said about saving the army.

That is the way of war.

Among those who did not believe it was Bonnie Dixon, who had strangled an Indian on the ground and caught the dragging war rope of a pony. His cynical attitude was to cost him dearly later.

Major Larkins came back, too, but he was dead when a trooper the major once had saved from a court-martial laid him on the ground behind the wagons. The private looked toward Montell and cursed bitterly; he was, however, just an uncouth recruit, hard to discipline and entirely ignorant of the beautiful traditions of stirrup-to-stirrup fighting.

The Indians might have carried their charge clear through the wagons and ridden up the green valley to demoralize the attacks against the hills. But they spent a good deal of time with the dead and wounded on the plain. They yelled and whooped and boasted. They searched for friends and brothers and carried them away. They were flushed with victory and quite disorderly. When Iron Buffalo and the other chiefs finally got part of them interested in a charge to crash through the lower end of the valley, the sheets of fire that came by platoons from behind the supply train was more than the Indians cared to face head-on.

Iron Buffalo gave a good demonstration of a man trying to get killed, though it was against his better judgment. He swept close to the wagons, firing as he rode. He shouted insults and waved his rifle and tried to get the others to come in for a charge. The Indians loved it. They loved Iron Buffalo, too, but they did not care to gallop straight into that steady, controlled fire.

So they withdrew and engaged in long-range skirmishing, which didn't cost either side too many casualties—unless you want to call thirty-one dead, brown and white, a great loss.

General Montell watched the Indians for a while and began to feel better. He sent a message to Old Stub: *Holding firm, after suffering losses while making dispositions.*

Old Stub said two words: "Murdering bastard!"

Lieutenant Collins said nothing. He nodded earnestly.

Rafe Winburn and the couriers coming toward the army heard the artillery. The tanned neck in front of Winburn twisted. "Maybe we can still get in."

The other messenger nodded.

A few minutes later they saw Iron Buffalo's cavalry debouch from the trees. The brothers stopped their tired horses.

"Looks like we don't get to Old Stub just yet," Winburn said. He studied the hills on the right until he found a familiar landmark of rock pinnacles.

Eight or ten Indians who had been galloping their ponies along the outside of the formation ahead saw the blue riders and came streaking toward them.

"Right at the foot of that middle pinnacle on our right is some old prospect holes," Winburn said. "Good place to stand off most anything."

The Indians gained rapidly. They got within shooting range just as the couriers' sobbing horses reached the trees. A bullet chopped into the hind leg of the animal Winburn was riding. He leaned out and back to look at the wound. It wasn't a bad one, but the horse was dead tired, and now its stride was broken. Still, they had a pretty good lead. There was a chance of making it.

As the horse faltered more and more, Winburn knew there was no chance for the animal as long as it was carrying double.

The other rider was holding up to stay close.

"Follow this gulch right to the bottom of that middle steeple!" Winburn freed his pistol. "The middle steeple!" A moment later he grunted. "I'm bad hit."

He tried to light on his good leg. The way he bounced and rolled when his wounded leg had to take part of the jar helped convince the couriers that he really was badly wounded. They hesitated and started to pull up.

The Indians whooped. Bullets made their cat-spit through the trees. The brothers went on.

Winburn rolled over and checked his pistol. There had been a time when he could take spills like this and come up grinning. Now he ached clear through, and his head was not clearing very fast. But he got the first Indian's pony.

The rest veered away from a direct course into the

trees. One of them began to yell and signal. They dismounted and entered the thicket in a natural skirmish line.

They didn't expose themselves much. Winburn missed two running shots. His targets whooped and jeered.

He hoped he might get one at least before they closed.

But he knew they would circle around him and come in from all sides. He saw them starting the move. He ran up the little gulch, kneeling now and then to fire. He'd had only fifteen cartridges in his gun and pockets, and water and mud hadn't done them any good. One of every four misfired.

He kept running. He continued to shoot. His wounded leg was paining badly now. The young warriors began to expose themselves more. Older ones, he knew, would have killed him without risk. These youngsters were determined to close in. Before long they all knew that he had only a pistol. They stayed low, leaping from one tree to another, bounding from the cover of one rock to the next.

They yelled derisively when Winburn shot and missed. Now that they were sure of their quarry, they didn't bother to shoot.

Well, Winburn thought, he'd come awful close to reaching Old Stub. All a man could do was try like hell, and when his luck petered out there was no use to whine. If those two kids had paid attention to what he yelled about the middle steeple, by now they should be just about to the old home some fool had started on a bull quartz seam straight into the cliff.

He ran a few paces farther and fired again. After the next shot he had two cartridges left. They both missed fire. He shifted the gun to his left hand and drew his knife. If those two kids knew enough to kill their horses in front of that hole . . .

The young men closed in.

Winburn's mud-streaked gray hair was whipping from side to side as he tried to watch the whole circle. He finally got his Indian before they clubbed him down.

Behind a dead horse neatly felled across the entrance to a prospect hole the brothers heard the whooping. One looked at the other. "He did a lot of shooting down there to be hurt as bad as we thought."

All the shells that had been coming at Billy Munro's back, each one aimed at him as an individual, suddenly had ceased, but Munro continued to lie on his stomach under the rim of the south mesa. He couldn't have told exactly how he'd got there beside Dan Beavers and Johannes. He was wet to the waist from wading the creek, but he couldn't remember any details, except that there had been a lot of shouting and shells had been exploding all around.

Beavers was talking. For all the change there was in his voice he might have been slouching along in the column or standing around a campfire.

"Them guns behind us have blowed up, or else they ran out of ammunition—or maybe they got sense enough to be cooling them." He looked across the valley. "They're trying to work up to another rush over on that flat."

"To hell with that one," Johannes said. "We got our own just over the hill."

Munro didn't say anything. Neither did he look around.

He did watch when Beavers said a regiment from the rear was charging a million Indians. He watched until the dust became so heavy he couldn't tell what was happening. Then he saw two great formations of Indians break out of the trees behind the tiny blue horsemen that had charged out on the plain. He swallowed hard and started to get sick.

Beavers said in a puzzled tone. "Where'd *they* come from?"

"They were hiding in the trees!" Munro's anger made him feel a little better.

"I don't mean the big bunches." Beavers was looking diagonally along the hill toward the mesa.

After a while Munro saw what he meant. Twenty or thirty blue-clad riders apparently had come out of the thickets near the bottom of the left H-leg. Shooting sounded heavy behind them. The cavalrymen went over the edge of the hill, dismounted and began to lead their horses down.

"You know something?" Beavers had raised up a little. "They look like Indians from here." After a while he said: "By God! They *are* Indians!"

Johannes said: "By God! You're right!" and then he yelled the news to brown-faced Sergeant Mullins, who was looking dourly at his men lying in a ragged line. The sergeant was trying to determine in advance which of them he would have to kick in the rump to get them started over the rim when the time came.

"So they was Indians!" Mullins yelled. "We're infantry!"

That sounded quite reasonable to Munro, but he kept puzzling over the statement, trying to find something wrong with it.

Beavers grinned. "You don't mind if we watch what they're up to, do you, Mullins?"

"Watch the hell out of 'em!" the sergeant yelled. He

had problems. Three of them were pretty close to him. He knew by the way they hid their heads and lay as though dead.

It didn't take long before Beavers and Johannes announced what the blue-uniformed Indians were planning. Somehow they had led their troopers' horses down one of the steep parts of the mesa side. They mounted and swam across a beaver pond.

"They're going to stampede the herd before anyone down there catches on!" Beavers said.

He was right. The picket guards had seen the riders come off the hill. They had seen lots of blue men riding in many directions in the last half hour. Two pickets were dead before the others caught on and began to shoot. They got four Indians.

The Indians got the horse herd.

Major O'Meara had come off the hill and was quite busy getting his regiment placed behind the supply wagons. The Indians in uniforms taken from Freeland's dead drove most of the herd through a large gap between the bottom of the right H-leg and the flank of the wagon fort.

"I don't like to think where they got them uniforms." Dan Beavers' red-stubbled face was grim. He looked at Munro, whose face was about as white as it could get.

Munro didn't say anything. He started to gulp again.

Beavers reached over and hit him so hard on the back that Munro cursed angrily. Then he saw Beavers was grinning.

"Pretty soon, Billy Boy, we're going for them trees across the flat," Beavers said. "Getting up to start will be your hardest part. After that, for a while anyway, you won't know what the hell you're doing. Stay close to me and Johannes." He grinned. "A red scalp like mine is quite a prize. You might have to save me."

Johannes grinned. "If they get me, Billy, don't let 'em scalp my beard. I got so little on top they might be sore."

Billy Munro grinned a little. His lips and cheeks felt stiff, but he tried hard to grin.

Sergeant Mullins saw. He took a doubtful off his list. Then, not liking inaction on the field even though no men of his were being killed, the sergeant said: "Let's pepper them hills where the guns are!" He called a list of names. ". . . and the rest of you! Crawl up a little!"

Munro went along with Beavers and Johannes. When he got his first close look at the purple mesa it seemed a mile wide. After a while he began to shoot with the others. A little later he even began to aim at the rock points above the green. He saw small branches jerk. Bullets bit little chips from the high rocks, then sang their eerie song until a tree stopped them or they fell from exhaustion. Firing began to build up all along the line of blue men spread just under the mesa rim for three hundred yards on each side of the crossbar of the H.

Light artillery did not reply. Indian riflemen did. Bullets splashed the edge of the mesa as large rain drops made dust leap. A large percentage was high. Some were not. Withdrawn below the rim to reload, Munro saw an infantryman's head jerk back as though someone had straight-armed a hard palm against the man's forehead.

For several moments Munro looked at the still figure and fumbled with his cartridge. Then he went up and fired.

Oversweep from the thickets carried into the valley, where almost-spent bullets now and then struck litter bearers bringing in wounded. A ball bounced off the projecting knuckle of Lieutenant Collins' right wrist. He had galloped from the shelter of the hill while Old Stub was busy talking to one of Gross's aides. Collins gave a stirrup to a wounded man who had been staggering and falling. The pair came to shelter slowly.

Though his fingers were numb and considerable blood had run down the back of his hand and was dripping from his little finger, Collins knew he was not hurt.

Finished with one side, Old Stub studied his own. The quick dark eyes took in everything. "Suppose I'd needed a dispatch, Collins?"

Collins nodded toward a clean-shaved, scared young second lieutenant. "Maybe, sir. He's very capable. Besides, I couldn't have written with my fingers numb."

Old Stub's eyes bored at the bloody hand. "Your fingers wouldn't be numb if you'd stayed where you belong," he growled.

Lieutenant Mayne's look at Collins conveyed sympathy for one about to be shot for running away from duty.

"Yes, sir," Collins said meekly. "Now that I'm useless, may I go up the hill?" He nodded toward the south.

Old Stub's face was severe. "Yes."

Mayne stared at the departing back in wonder. For a moment he didn't hear Old Stub's next sentence. Maybe he didn't hear it at all.

"I think he bit that hand," the general said.

"Yes, sir," Mayne said mechanically.

Collins dipped his wrist in the icy creek while wading across. Except for tingling, his fingers were almost normal when he came under the rim behind Munro and his companions.

"We must be making it hot for those gunners," Beaver said. "I haven't seen anything move on the high points."

His eyesight was excellent. Soon after the raking fire began from the mesa edge the gunners had pulled their pieces off the rocks and were now taking them apart. Neither rifle fire nor lack of ammunition had caused the move. They had plenty of ammunition, but it was all for twelve-pound guns.

All the twelve-pounders were on the north hills, where Cannibal Bullard was raging because all he had left was two-pound ammunitions and some balls for the worthless Wiard. Tolerant souls might have forgiven the Indians for their mistake. Their white brothers, long-used to large killing devices like cannons, had been making similar errors for centuries.

Simon Bullard forgave nobody.

He bellowed and cursed until the Indians looked at him in amazement. He was a strange man, but brave. Hadn't he ridden alone through the entire army of blue soldiers to make sure they had no cannons hidden in their wagons?

Cannibal Bullard, slyly known as Eats People among his brother Crows, ordered the guns taken down and carried away, including the little two-pounders that still had ammunition. Two-pounders are not large. Even the hot barrels were easy to handle on their pole litters, with four Indians carrying a mere 120 pounds of Whitworth steel. That, too, was all the carriage weighed, while each wheel was barely more than fifty pounds.

The twelve-pounders gave a little more trouble. Their barrels weighed more than 200 pounds. However, the Indians didn't have to take them far to a road of sorts that Iron Buffalo had caused to be made in a little gulch. Bullard stayed with the guns until he was sure the young Navajos he left in charge knew what to do. Not that they hadn't practiced many times.

When the barrels were cool enough, mules with pack frames kindly supplied by Washington would take the two-pounders over the mountains. The heavier guns would be assembled and pulled away by other mules, also gifts of a benign and careless War Department.

Bullard did not overlook the ammunition.

When he had bellowed his last order concerning the guns and ammunition, he went running through the trees to join two crews manning Gatling guns on the hill above the top of the right H-leg. In spite of his great size Bullard was swift. He didn't make a great crashing as he ran.

More than one Indian watching the mesa below looked uneasy as the huge black-bearded man sped past. In addition to their awe at someone who was not quite sane, the Indians always were a little startled at any sudden appearance of Cannibal Bullard.

The attack across the south mesa was delayed, which meant that blue men did not rise from the shelter of a hillside and sprint into an open space to receive the sudden thump of lead as soon as they might have.

Eventually officers below the rim became quite sure that both flanks were engaged. There was no mistake this time. An infantry brigadier in one of the widest gullies gave the first order.

Soldiers went onto the mesa in little groups, twenty-five here, forty to the left or right a hundred yards away, then little bunches in the middle. The attack was not so planned, but the lack of a co-ordinated surge saved many lives. Indian fire veered wildly and was not nearly as effective as it might have been.

Billy Munro ran between Beavers and Johannes. Sergeant Mullins was not far behind. He had been obliged to kick only three men over the rim to get them started. One of them was killed quickly, but the other two went on. Mullins had time to think that justice had been done: the dead sulker had been a cowardly bastard who had tried to run back to the sheltering rim. That one of the others took a shot in the groin and bled to death quickly before reaching the trees Mullins did not have time to consider.

Munro's mouth was dry. He was yelling and barely conscious of the fact. He knew that he had been running a long time and that the trees were far away. He shot his half-raised Springfield. He cocked it and pulled the trigger again.

"Load it, kid!" Beavers yelled. "Then wait!"

Munro heard. He even tried to obey. It made him angry to think that Beavers had been watching him even as they ran. The trees came closer. Then he was among them lying down. Right in front of his face was a small aspen twig with a few leaves and a bullet-severed stem. He knocked it away savagely, as though it blocked his view of all the trees ahead.

He raised his rifle and tried a shot. The heavy hammer came down. No more.

"They use bullets," Beavers said. Already he had shot twice and was rolling on one elbow to reload from a handful of cartridges laid before him on the ground. He'd lost his cap. His hair was dark red against the gray trunks around them and the green and silver leaves above them.

Munro began to load and fire into the smoke ahead. After a while he began to aim at what he convinced himself must be movement. There was a fearful hell of smoke and sound and viperous whisk of lead coming from the thicket, but so far he had not seen an Indian.

"See how he is," Beavers said.

Munro stared. "See—who?"

"Johannes."

Munro had forgotten Johannes lying to the right. Now he saw that the soldier's head was down, with overflow from Johannes' black beard showing beyond his collar. Munro shook him. "Hey, Johannes!" Blue wool was warm in Munro's fingers. Johannes' body moved loosely as he shoved.

He had been shot squarely in the mouth, and the ball had torn a great hole in the back of his neck.

Munro looked wide-eyed at Beavers. "He's dead!"

Beavers nodded. "Shoot, kid."

"I'll just take his gun and shells," someone lying behind Munro said. The fellow crawled ahead.

Munro saw it was the lieutenant from Old Stub's headquarters. He had a handkerchief tied around one wrist. Blood was smeared on his long yellow mustache from pulling one of the ends with his teeth. He took Johannes' rifle and cartridge box.

Munro couldn't take his eyes off the lieutenant. He didn't belong here, somehow. This was a whole lot different from hanging around the general's headquarters all the time.

Yet the lieutenant didn't seem to mind. He acted like Beavers. Mechanically Munro put another cartridge in the breach.

"How'd you get away from Old Stub?" Beavers asked.

Collins loaded Johannes' rifle deftly. "He fired me."

Iron Buffalo soon saw that the Indians were not going to ride through the wagon fort. With heavy loss among the first waves they could have carried through, but that was not the Indian way. Much of his leadership had slipped away, as he had known it would. He acted to regain a part of it.

While a great many Indians capered before the wagons, just out of range except for daring souls who rode close to shoot from under the necks of their ponies—frequently getting unhorsed or killed during the exhibition—Iron Buffalo and Bad Jaw rounded up some chiefs to send young men after the captured horse herd.

That move under way, Iron Buffalo paused to read sun signals from above the north mesa. He and Bad Jaw prevailed upon the other chiefs to gather six or seven hundred warriors who rode at once toward the trees above the bottom of the right H-leg. Neither Fighting Bear nor Iron Buffalo had been blind when Montell recalled O'Meara from flanking the lower end of that hill.

Not long after the attack on the south hills started, Bad Jaw led his force to the edge of the trees and scouted the bottom of the right H-leg. Most of the soldiers who had been repulsed in their first attempt to cross the north mesa were concentrated close to the gullies. Bad Jaw's warriors left their ponies in the trees and raced across the lower end of the flat. The range was long, but they had good rifles. They lay down and began to drop an effective fire on the left flank of Montell's wagon fort.

General Montell did not long remain unaware of this development, not after a splinter from an axle bolster ripped a gash in his massive forehead. He wavered between pulling in his left flank or sending part of his force to take the hill. Then the Indians in front feinted a mighty charge. Far beyond them dust was billowing from what appeared to be a new force. Montell sat and wavered.

His left flank was held by engineers, cooks, musicians, wagon drivers, blacksmiths and wounded. It was two hundred feet short of reaching the bottom of the hill, a weakness that some of his staff had pointed out. Montell had been too busy with other plans to act upon their suggestions.

Bad Jaw's command began to enjoy their work. Even a few Comanches who had been reluctant to dismount began to appreciate the sport of shooting from the edge of a hill, with practically no risk to themselves. They killed Montell's beloved horses. They killed his men.

Bulwarked behind bags of rice and flour, Montell sat and cursed bitterly the incompetence of the man who had got them into this frightful mess.

He quit cursing only when he saw the charge forming in front was not a feint this time.

A mile away at the head of the valley, Major-General Gross lowered his binoculars and acted to relieve Montell. Gross had been holding the valley with Colonel Accola's regiment, dismounted and lying in an arc that bent into the valley to concentrate fire. Now Gross had part of a second regiment—Colonel Matthews'.

About three-fourths of Matthews' regiment and the advance party had returned after a running retreat. They had barely missed getting slaughtered in a trap identical to the one Montell had sent Major Larkins into. Only the sound sense of the advance party major and overeagerness on the part of some young Shoshoni had saved the regiment. All the way back the three blue formations had lost men.

The blocks of Gross's prone carbineers showed themselves high enough not to be trampled, received their returning comrades through wide intervals and stopped the pursuers with careful fire.

Gross made a quick shift. He replaced his blocks of prostrate men with those who had returned on wind-blown horses. He sent Colonel Accola's regiment flying down the valley. That left the lumpish, black-jowled German with a line precariously held. No one knew it better than he. But he had stood with his pale eyebrows drawn low and watched a superior force recoil from controlled fire. It had been the first Indian charge he'd ever seen. He had learned something about Indians from it.

He had one other advantage. On his left a huge beaver dam spread almost a fourth of the way across the valley and made soggy ground even farther. That shortened his line and helped considerably.

The rest was hope.

In front of him he estimated there were thirty-five hundred Indian cavalry. His estimate was just two hundred high. General Gross, whose only interest outside the military was horticulture, did not care for glory or heroics; but he believed that battles should be won if there was any way they could be won. At the moment, it appeared to him that the worst threat was the flanking attack against Montell's *wagenburg*.

Old Stub saw Accola's regiment galloping down the valley and read the movement accurately. He ordered his only reserve battalion of infantry to get out of the river, where they had been getting thoroughly wet and muddy while building little mud walls to protect themselves against renewal of artillery fire. He sent the battalion up the valley to reinforce Gross's line. He had planned to send them to Montell, but Gross's quick action was solving that problem.

While Colonel Accola's regiment was going down the valley, the second attack across the north mesa began.

Now the whole army was engaged. Action would reach the crisis soon.

Old Stub's short gray beard pointed one way and then another. He could only watch and wait.

General Montell kept Accola in conference behind the rice and flour while the colonel's dismounted regiment began to lose horses from the fire off the mesa. Finally the general ordered Accola to take his regiment out on the plain and disrupt the attack forming there, warning him not to become "too heavily involved," which proved that Montell had learned at least a little by throwing away eight hundred men.

Accola did not salute. As well as becoming careless of military courtesy, he seemed to have developed a stoppage of the ears. He took his dismounted regiment straight up the side of the hill and dislodged Bad Jaw's force. The troopers were unable to go onto the mesa because a Gatling gun flamed prematurely from a hill and held the attack below the rim.

Colonel Accola's regiment controlled the rim and swapped fire with Bad Jaw's dwindling force, which had retreated to the trees. More than half of them mounted and rode back to the plain to get in on the riding attack that was being formed by Iron Buffalo.

That charge came shortly after the left flank of the wagon fort had been relieved.

Driving before them the captured herd, the Indians thundered straight at the wagons. They rode low behind the riderless mounts. They held their fire and came in five great waves obscured by dust. Soldiers holding the *wagenburg* began to kill the animals. Horses went down in grotesque spins and lunges, others trampled them or fell. Now and then sure-footed ponies were caught by the jam and fell, sending their riders spinning through the dusty air. Like maddened beasts with a common grievance the herd roared toward the wagons. For a moment it seemed that the rolling thunder of shod hoofs and sheer weight of pulsing flesh would crush the wagons.

A few soldiers rose and ran.

The herd tried to turn. Most of them did. Some were thrown forward by pressure and their own momentum and were crippled or killed against the wagons. Others streamed through the gaps and ran wildly up the valley, and one surging mass jammed in a passage between wagons. Horses behind them piled up. A white mare screamed in terror as pressure and her own leap carried her up on the backs of the struggling jam. She rolled on her side and fell to the ground only when the terrified horses overturned two wagons and broke free.

Officers' luggage spilled on the ground. A trooper dragged a case in front of him and used it as protection.

The initial wave of riders behind the herd fired their first shots. Lead splintered into the wagons, sang from iron rims and bolts. General Montell hunched lower behind his stores. Less valuable, more exposed men clenched their teeth and returned the fire.

To Trooper Bonnie Dixon, one-time divinity student, lately returned from the slaughter of Larkins' regiment, it seemed that the whole first wave of Indians had been shot from their horses. But in an instant most of them reappeared. They swerved their horses toward his left, toward the wide gap between the flank of the wagons and the hill.

Dixon took careful sight at a chief in the next wave. He shot just as the line of Indians was masked by their own volley. Whether or not he had got the chief he couldn't tell. The second wave went over the sides of their horses and streaked for the wide gap.

Looking through the V of wagon spokes and trying to reload quickly for the next wave, Dixon felt a patter of what seemed like hot blood on the back of his neck. After he fired again he shifted a little to the side. The tiny pelting blows continued on his back and shoulders.

His back crawled. He had no time to move or even look above him. He reloaded to fire again.

From the elevation of the hill, Colonel Accola saw the Indians' strategy. After each volley the attackers were veering to pour into that gap. If they turned the flank and got behind the wagons . . .

An unknown captain of engineers had seen, too. He had been standing high on a wagon seat to watch the charge. No one could hear his voice, but he made his arms talk as he waved and pointed. Those on the left flank got ready.

On the hill all but a hundred of Accola's men ran down to shorten range. "Low! Hold low!" the order ran.

Iron Buffalo was the first man through the gap. He spun his pony and brandished his rifle high, signaling for those behind to turn along the unprotected rear of the wagons.

The first main body of Indians, mainly Sioux, hit the breech.

As though by one command, those sprawled along the flank of the wagons and those on the hill fired into the mass. Scores of dead or crippled ponies litttered the gap. A surprisingly large number of Indians held their feet in running leaps and tried to catch loose ponies belonging to those who had no further need of horses. After the first searing volley, shooting became an individual matter. It was scarcely less deadly than the initial blast. Even so, a large part of the second wave carried through the gap, though many were on foot.

Iron Buffalo tried to turn his followers along the rear of the wagons. Once locked in close combat with the blue men, he knew the fire from the hill would have to stop. He was succeeding until his pony fell dead under him. He leaped clear. His bad knee made him stagger to hands and knees. By a hair he missed being trampled by a frantic wounded pony. He caught the dragging war rope of another and mounted.

The brief loss of time ruined his plans.

He had turned part of the Indians. But the full force that could have been exerted by those who rode through was dissipated. Some rode whooping to capture Accola's horses. Small groups went wild and galloped straight up the valley for individual reasons. One large group of Comanches rode along the base of the hill, firing at the soldiers above them.

Impeded greatly by the tangled litter of dead ponies, the third wave hit the breech. They took a terrible crossfire. A few more than half got through.

No one realized better than Iron Buffalo that his people's age-old aversion to fighting on foot in the open was going to serve them badly. He dismounted and led all he could command against the wagon flank in close struggle.

Empty rifle against empty rifle, knife to knife, bare arms and blue arms choking, striking, swinging weapons—the fight surged among the wagons.

A little phalanx of Oglala and Brule persisted in staying in front of Iron Buffalo. Most of them were killed. Shots ripped the smoke and chunked into close-locked bodies. Indians and soldiers went down fighting, some not realizing the man they wrestled with was dead.

In front of the fort the fourth and fifth waves of warriors, the bulk of the force that had charged behind the cavalry herd, carried out their plan by lying prone and keeping the blue defenders from turning to relieve their flank.

From the trees across the north mesa Bad Jaw led a charge to strike Accola's regiment from the rear. The colonel had anticipated the move. The hundred men he'd left under the rim broke the rush before it got well started. Bad Jaw could not get his men to try that open space again.

The captain of engineers who had foreseen the Indians' strategy pulled forty infantrymen with bayoneted rifles from under the wagons on the front line. Over the bewildered objections of their officers, he got the men by roars and the drive of a commanding personality.

Appropriately enough, the engineer had armed himself with a shovel. He led the infantry in a rush to bolster the bending flank. One company came leaping off the hill to help.

Iron Buffalo read the handwriting. He didn't have to call a retreat. It was under way already.

The Indians who had scattered in the valley met bad luck. Those who tried to stampede the horses of the regiment on the hill found the holders hard to handle. The horses did stampede, but they went up instead of down the valley. A few hardy Assiniboines who had explored far away saw how the fight had turned. They had to abandon their horses to escape up the north mesa side.

Iron Buffalo retreated with the rest. He took a wounded Oglala with him.

The attack, he knew, had gone to pieces while he was

catching a loose pony after losing his zigzagged brown favorite.

Peering between the wagon spokes, Bonnie Dixon drew a fine bead on a retreating Minneconjou. Someone on the hill killed the pony just before Dixon was ready to shoot. He shifted his muzzle a touch and got the Indian who left the dead animal before it hit the ground. That was the first enemy he was sure of, though he had several possibles on his list. He couldn't be sure that he had throttled the Cheyenne out on the plain with Larkins.

With detached clarity Dixon reflected that one sure dead enemy was a large contribution. If every man on each side killed one opponent—well, there wouldn't be a man alive on the entire field.

Bonnie Dixon relaxed. He had time now to look at that loathsome drip that had made his back crawl.

It was rice leaking through a crack in the wagon boards.

Less than two hundred seconds had passed between the time Iron Buffalo led the charge through the gap and then raced away with the wounded Oglala in front of him. Between the flank they almost had rolled back and the hill, his warriors had lost five to one. But even under the crossfire they had borne away nearly a hundred dead or wounded, almost one fourth of their casualties.

Apaches, Crows, Snakes and others who had crept close to the wagons to fire from behind dead horses began to withdraw. Except for long-range work the battle at the *wagenburg* was finished.

Killing all the Indians not yet dead among the upthrust legs and bleeding bodies of the ponies was merely routine. Some who were crawling quite a distance away offered competition between sharpshooters trying to pick them off and Indian riders dashing in to lift their comrades from the ground without dismounting.

The little skirmish was over.

Montell was standing now, looking quite heroic and military, except for flour smears on his back. He had been rather quiet during the fighting. In fact he hadn't made an outburst since he first saw Accola disobeying orders. But, since things had turned out the way they had, Montell decided he could be generous about that.

Then, in a sudden flash of inspiration for which he was noted, Montell decided that he had made a rather remarkable decision in ordering Colonel Accola to occupy that hill.

He sent a message to Old Stub: *Have repulsed all attacks. Holding firm. Need reinforcements.*

Old Stub sent Lieutenant Mayne with: *Your reinforcements lying straight ahead of you. Continue to hold firm.*

Montell puzzled for a time over the message. His natural sneer came into full bloom again. Let the old peasant indulge in his crude humor. Those "reinforcements" had saved the army. Yes, that master stroke of boldness had been costly, but worth the sacrifice. The regiment had died gloriously. Even the magnificent horses!

But someone, Montell thought grimly, would have to have a court for letting the savages steal the horse herd. The stupid guards should have known at a glance that the thieves were savages in troopers' uniforms. Montell had known, right after an aide had shouted that some of the riders were throwing away forage caps and stripping off blue coats.

That had been after the Indians were in the clear with the herd.

Coming in against the Indians' flank at the top of the left H-leg, Gross's Second Brigade met light resistance. The soldiers flushed fifty or sixty leaping brown men from the trees and fired at them enthusiastically.

Then the front ranks of the advance, extended three hundred yards up the hill from the edge of the mesa, came to a sharp, bare little spine of granite that ran up and down the hill. Trees were thin on top of the rib. There was an open space of approximately fifty feet on the far side of the little spine.

Men began to pile up against the near side, peering over cautiously and waiting for the comforting support of more blue soldiers. They heard the right flank of their line get into heavy going somewhere up the hill. Men turned their faces in a fruitless effort to see what was going on.

The uphill firing grew heavier and heavier.

Those below had a job to do, and it was straight ahead. Noncoms listened to officers. Troopers listened to noncoms. The line went up and over the hill.

When blue was thick on the little bare ridge, two Gatling guns sent their twenty-barreled murder from a rock point up the hill. Men twisted, fell, leaped and ran. In a short time the spine was clear of those who could move.

Some made it to the trees on the far side. Those on the near side stopped where there was cover. They didn't want to leave protection. But they tried again when Major Friskey, who was either a poor historian or facetious, waved a sword and cried: "Remember the Alamo!"

He rushed to stand on top the spine and waved for others to follow.

When the ridge swarmed with blue again the Gatlings raked it lengthwise. For just an instant the two guns reached their maximum of one thousand rounds per minute. Powerful as their wrists and shoulders were, the Ute and Navajo gunners could not take capacity firing vibrations from the cranks for more than a few seconds.

Seconds were enough.

Major Friskey did not fall. He was one of those who went back to the near side. He lived a long time. He lived to get his colonelcy and be referred to by his bored grandchildren as "that damned old Indian killer."

He went upon the ridge a third time and urged men to follow. This time he did not sound his war cry. That may have been why so few joined him. The Gatlings did not flame at him because the gunners did not care to waste their wonderful fire on a dozen men. They had learned well from Cannibal Bullard. Even in the heat of battle some of the gunners carried an uneasy feeling that the huge, wild-eyed man would leap roaring from nowhere if they forgot his lessons.

Before the guns were nearly a hundred Shawnees and Delawares to take care of rifle work. Snug in the rocks on the left flank were three hundred Utes. The heavy firing soldiers farther down the hill had heard was the result of their right flank encountering the Utes. That end of the line was pinned down by the fire straight ahead and blocked by a little cliff rising on the troopers' right. In the trees beyond the top of that cliff were a hundred or more Bannock riflemen.

With the two Gatlings controlling almost the full

sweep of rock spine, the flanking attack was badly stalled.

A captain told Major Friskey rather bluntly: "We'll have to get those guns before any more of my men go out there."

The major agreed, still somewhat shaken to think that so many soldiers were craven enough to want to go on living when they could have joined him on the ridge in glory.

Between them the two officers got two hundred men started up the hill to reinforce the right flank and sweep around the guns. High on the little cliff a Bannock chief spotted the movement. He sent an arrow arching above the thickets. It wobbled in flight because the two bone whistles on the shaft were not evenly balanced. The arrow made an eerie, penetrating noise. It brought a hundred and fifty Piutes bounding to reinforce the Bannocks above the cliff.

Outnumbered, fighting against a brutal disadvantage of terrain, the right flank of the blue line was unable to get close to the guns.

To those below, on either side of the rocky spine, the location of the guns was no secret. Smoke was still thick around the top of a little hill of shattered granite. The acrid gas was not escaping very fast because of thick pine logs blocking the muzzle ends of two narrow gaps between slabs of rock. At the tops of the logs, which leaned inward against the gaps, two long poles were lashed with rawhide ropes. The poles extended from the log ends back over the top of the rocks, to where more rawhide ropes went straight down into the hands of Ute and Navajo hoistmen.

By bearing down on their end of the poles and moving sideways, the operators could walk the heavy logs away from the Gatling muzzles.

The arrangement was simple enough, not nearly as complicated as a bow and scarcely any more intricate than a *travois*.

Those logs, the protecting riflemen and a cuplike recess on top the shattered hill made the guns secure.

Simon Bullard couldn't have placed them one bit better.

The gunners were fortunate in having those heavy logs, for enraged soldiers in the trees below sent such a cone of fire against the hill that bullets thumped by fours and fives into the thick trunks, while countless others screamed from rocks.

A few lieutenants had small groups across the spine in staggered rushes. For a few moments the movement became general, if not popular. Then the logs walked. Two short bursts killed twenty-five men while too many rifles had been diverted from the hill.

Most of the two regiments had not crossed the little ridge. Major Friskey had made the grade. From the trees on the far side he called for men to follow, until creeping Santees and Arapahos sent lead to find him by sound. The major lay low, but he didn't stop cursing.

Meanwhile, those who had attacked frontally across the mesa were making little progress up the hill. The first fifty or sixty yards was not bad. Then, without support from either flank, the center bogged down. All who hadn't been deafened temporarily by a comrade's firing too close to their ears knew why the flanks were not getting in.

They had heard the rolling thunder from both sides.

Down in the valley Old Stub heard. He heard the same venomous rattling coming from the hill above the top of the right H-leg also, where Gross's Fourth Brigade was having bloody trouble. Up there Cannibal Bullard was proud of the Nez Percé gunners cranking and loading the two Gatlings that were stopping Gross's Fourth Brigade, with plenty of help from well-concealed Tontos and Kiowas.

Bullard's battery didn't have a little ridge to sweep, but lead had made a lane in the thicket, a lane where silver and green aspen leaves fluttered to rest on blue that was wet with blood.

Old Stub didn't know about the single Gatling above the bottom of the right H-leg. It had made only one short, too-soon burst against Colonel Accola's men when they were driving Bad Jaw's force back across the mesa. The general's face was bleak enough without knowing about that gun. To him men were not statistics, and he had seen Gatling guns demonstrated. The last time had been in Denver when the Power was taking him on a tour of the fortifications.

"Dust off those observors out there!" the Power had ordered a lieutenant.

The observors, four Cheyennes sitting on their ponies a mile away on a hill, had been fascinated by the noise of the Gatling, if not its range. They had stayed on the hill until the gunner's arms were numb and the gun was too hot to shoot.

These Gatlings in the trees above him, Old Stub knew, were firing at terribly effective range.

On the south hill Lieutenant Collins peered over a rock to look at the distant point of granite on his right, from which smoke was curling. He could see more smoke on the little cliff behind the guns, where Bannocks and Piutes were supporting the Utes below.

"That carbuncle up there needs a lancing," Collins said.

Sergeant Mullins glared at the lieutenant in complete agreement.

"Get ten good men, Sergeant."

Among the ten were Beavers and Munro. There was an eleventh, a gray-haired, stooped man. His mouth was full of tobacco juice but his "The hell you say, son!" was quite plain when Collins shook his head and offered: "*You* don't have to go, Babcock."

Thirteen men backed down the hill and began to run low in the edge of the thickets, going toward the top of the left H-leg. Ten were left when they neared the lower end of a little rocky spine that pointed straight up the hill toward the two Gatlings.

"How we going to do it?" Mullins asked.

"I haven't the least idea," Collins said. "You see, I'm new at this sort of thing."

Mullins grunted a little. He was getting used to Lieutenant Collins. If he would only cut off that damn fool mustache, he might amount to something after all.

Old Stub, Major-General Gross and Iron Buffalo knew how completely the army was checked. Old Fighting Bear, huddled behind the high point of his granite hill, was well aware of the fact.

Old Stub was sure the Indians would not leave their solid positions on the hills and come down for knee-to-knee fighting—not unless one or both of the large cavalry masses ahead of and behind the army broke into the valley. The rear had held once. It could do the same again. Old Stub did not believe the Indians would try that gap again.

Now the danger lay in front. Old Stub had sent the last reserve battalion of infantry to help Gross.

The general waited, hoping the long quiet of the light artillery would continue.

Gross had used the reserve infantry well in strengthening his line across the upper end of the valley. Even so, he knew he was weak and covering too much open ground. If the cavalry ahead concentrated on his right flank against the base of the hill, they could break through, roll up his line and rocket down the valley to strike in force against the rear of the *wagenburg*. Then those who had been stopped once at the lower end of the valley would sweep in. Indians on the hills would get bolder. The battle would no longer be controlled by anyone. It would degenerate into individual dog fights, with the Indians holding a large advantage in mobility.

Gross tried to light a cigar. The wrapper was crackly dry, and the cigar was broken in the middle. He pulled it apart and lit one ragged end. Bulging, untidy, lumpish, he stood looking up the park. The end of the cigar flared fiercely. His eyes were almost closed.

"Vell," he said, "ve found the Indians."

A brigade headquarters captain nodded nervously, irritated a little by the German's heavy humor and the accent lapse.

Gross grinned like a pirate through the stench of his cigar. "I'm almost balt, Captain. You have a preddy head of hair. Nice for scalping, eh?"

The captain did not answer. He fought hard to overcome an urge to pull his hat down a little tighter.

Certain that he could not interest his cavalry in a second charge against the wagon fort, Iron Buffalo had ridden to the trees where Bad Jaw's men still were swapping shots with the soldiers just below the mesa edge. As far as Iron Buffalo could see, the battle was not lost yet.

Many-shooting guns on the south mesa had the soldiers stopped. Fighting Bear's mirror said the same about the attack on the top of the right H-leg. Peeping over a rock breastwork on a hill behind Iron Buffalo was another many-shooting gun to hold back the blue men who had spoiled the Indians' attempt to flank the wagon fort.

What Iron Buffalo did not know was that the gun behind him was jammed. Nobody knew that except its crew, and they didn't know why. A big Cayuse Indian might have known. He was the one who had slipped a handful of small stones into the Accles drum, hoping to hear the rocks whistle when they came from the barrels. The Cayuse rubbed the still-cool brass casings and was content.

In the trees below Iron Buffalo told a young Brule: "Go quickly to Fighting Bear. Tell him to send the sun to those far ahead. Tell them to ride over the soldiers who hold the upper end of the valley."

Like Gross and Old Stub, Iron Buffalo knew a weak spot when he saw one. He wondered why The Otter, strong-hearted, hot-blooded Shoshoni chief, had not attacked before.

Far up the park, demonstrating Indians saw the signals. Following the unco-ordinated scramble that had driven Matthews' regiment back, The Otter had tried to organize a full-scale smash against Gross's line, long before Old Stub's infantry reserves had arrived to reinforce the German. But The Otter had been balked by Red Bull, old Bannock chief, and others.

Controlling anger, The Otter spoke again. "Even with

their new soldiers we are more. Let us trample them into the grass. The walking soldiers who came last are in the middle with their long gun-knives. Let us strike hard near the hill where the riding soldiers have no long knives on their guns to rip our ponies."

Gross would have closed his eyes almost entirely to look with great respect upon The Otter if the stout German could have heard the chief's words.

Red Bull did not like the words. "We have killed many of the blue soldiers," he said. "I have shot five. Three in the rocks where the little army was. Two today." His listeners feared that he might relate the exploits of his two sons and all his nephews, not to mention a younger brother who had worn a war bonnet without the right. "Now the soldiers will go away. They have felt the power of the Bannocks." His listeners waited. Red Bull read their expressions. "And their brothers."

"Let us fight now and council afterward," The Otter said.

But some were of the same opinion as Red Bull, including Cuerno, the huge Ute chief, though the Utes and Shoshonis had once all been brothers living together.

The chiefs let the young men ride and shout at the soldiers. The chiefs went into council. They counciled a long time, for among them were more Montells than Grosses.

A thoughtful old warrior who was watching ponies built a fire of grass. He threw on some green blades and used his blanket to signal that the committee was in session.

Iron Buffalo already had feared as much.

Lying close to Sergeant Mullins, Lieutenant Collins

studied the hill they had to climb. Ahead of him and to his right, lying parallel with the rocky spine, were three or four hundred troopers who had crossed the little ridge. Now they were in the edge of the trees and they weren't going much farther without support. Thirty feet in front of the sprawled blue line two slopes met to form a little dry valley that had carried snow water from the hills for years beyond time.

Collins threw a careful study on the depression. It was not deep, though in places water had cut down to close-lying bedrock. Ferns and bushes edged the sides. If a man could keep his hind end down he might get up the little ditch a distance that depended on so many factors Collins didn't bother to consider them.

"The first thing," Mullins said, "is get acquainted with them cavalry on the right. They might not know red from blue. You can't trust cavalry too far."

Collins watched bushes jerking on both sides of the depression. The Indians and cavalrymen, he knew, were shooting more or less blindly at each other. Both were prone. They were putting bullets close above the ditch.

"Go over to those cavalrymen, Sergeant. Find someone with good sense—another sergeant, say. Have him crawl up their line and tell everybody to make it hot to cover us."

Mullins spoke without looking back as he crawled away. "After you get up a ways—then what?"

"I can't plan *that* far ahead." Without looking to see whether anyone was following, the lieutenant had started worming up the depression. Babcock was right behind him; then two cousins from Albany, New York; then Munro, Beavers and the rest. After a short distance they all paused to take off clumsy bayonets.

"Keep them big feet down, Billy," Beavers whispered.

"No bigger than yours," Munro said.

"Everybody shut up!" Babcock said.

Sergeant Mullins didn't bother to find anyone with good sense. He figured he had that himself. So he crawled behind the line of cavalrymen, lunging fast to cross little open spaces between rocks, telling everyone he passed: "Keep 'em down over there! There's a detail going after them guns!" To Sergeant Mullins a detail was a detail, whether it was loading stores on wagons or crawling just under murderous crossfire in the scant protection of a small waterway.

Most troopers did not even look around. They didn't want to take their eyes from the trees ahead, nor did they want to look toward wounded men moaning and crying out on the rock spine. Mullins' raspy voice carried authority. The few who saw he was an infantryman didn't care. Almost everyone obeyed. They laid down good protecting fire for Collins and the others.

Major Friskey examined Sergeant Mullins, desiring among other things to know who was leading the sneak up the little depression.

"Old Stub himself!" Mullins said. "He knew the cavalry was no good!" He paused. "Sir."

The major cleared his throat and started to rise in anger. A Flathead warrior who had had his eye on that pretty sword ever since he saw it flashing on the rocky spine almost got the owner. Major Friskey dropped back to cover.

Mullins went on. "Keep every red devil down . . ."

Before the sergeant got so close to the Shawnees and Delawares protecting the front of the guns that he could go no farther, he had caused Collins and his party to be well covered. Mullins had done all he could. Bushes and trees obscured the depression so he couldn't see into it. He hoped those above him couldn't either.

He tried to stop the flow of blood from his broken arm. The one ear that had been almost shot away was paining more than the arm. After eighteen years in the army Sergeant Mullins was used to oddities like that.

Mullins laid before him a pistol he had taken from a dead cavalryman. He pressed his thumb hard against the inside of his arm, under his shoulder, and watched the rocks ahead.

Without a sound one of the Shawnees came bounding from cover. He held an upraised bayonet. Someone behind Mullins yelled. He heard lead sing over his head. The Shawnee made four great leaps that carried him almost to Mullins. The sergeant picked up the pistol. His left hand was clumsy. It didn't matter. The cartridge misfired. The Shawnee reached Sergeant Mullins.

The bayonet went higher. It started down. Someone stepped on Mullins' legs. A sword flashed, and a third of its length went into the Indian's belly. He fell grunting beside Mullins, who beat his head in with the pistol.

Major Friskey, who had stepped on the sergeant's legs, to make his thrust, had proved a point: you could jab with a sword as well as slash. He wrote a manual about it afterward, and many years later he made a nuisance of himself by talking about the manual to his uninterested grandchildren, all of whom were girls.

Mullins made a deathless vow on the spot. Never again would he speak disparagingly of the cavalry, not even its officers. Of course he didn't live up to the vow, but it was a worthy thought.

With him the major had brought approximately thirty troopers, who promptly discouraged other Shawnees from coming out to get either Sergeant Mullins or their brother's body, which by now Mullins was using as a barricade behind which to determine how many bad rounds you could find in a cavalryman's pistol.

Well dug in, the Shawnees and Delawares shot carefully. They got one trooper through the throat. They caught another with a ball that ranged diagonally from his shoulder point to his bowels. Until blood choked him he rolled from side to side and screamed for someone to kill him.

Across the little depression other Indians crept in closer and began to kill and wound more soldiers.

"I hope your sword holds out better than this damned pistol," Mullins told the major. The sergeant really had no quarrel with the weapon. The faulty primer that had almost cost his life had been the only bad one in the gun.

"Who's down in that little trench?" Friskey asked.

In spite of a growing faintness from loss of blood, dour Sergeant Mullins spoke proudly. "A fine young lieutenant aide from Old Stub's headquarters and some of my own good boys."

It didn't hurt to use a few good words, Mullins thought. He didn't expect to get out of this anyway.

The fine young lieutenant aide had led his good boys as far as they could go. Collins was hard against a vertical granite rock that would sparkle with a little waterfall in spring. Foliage was thick on both sides of the depression. Bullets were sweeping through it, bruising green bark from aspens, flicking fern leaves aside.

Collins' mustache brushed the water-smoothed rock as he lifted his head to look toward the guns. He saw the logs and wondered at them. Just then they walked. Twenty barrels shot flame through smoke and fourteen blue men trying a quick dash across the rocky spine went down.

Lieutenant Collins lowered his head and twisted his neck to look back. "Babcock—"

Two Spokan Indians, one a chief in war bonnet, had rolled somehow into the depression. They had slit the throats of the two soldiers at the rear of the line. As Collins yelled, the chief got another soldier, who was looking at Collins to see what the shout was all about when the Spokan's knife struck a kidney.

The second Indian exposed himself above the depression for just an instant as he leaped toward Beavers. Lieutenant Collins tried to draw his side arm. He knew the lack of time made the act only a gesture, but he tried. He saw the Indian flat in the air above Beavers, poising a bloody knife. Then it seemed that all but the Spokan's head came down on the infantryman. Collins saw the strong, bronzed muscles of the Indian's throat bend back.

Lying on his back, Beavers had pivoted his rifle in both hands and jabbed the muzzle straight at the Spokan's face. The end had struck the Indian's mouth. His neck might have been broken then. Beavers pulled the trigger a split second later.

Scrabbling on hands and knees the chief cleared the body of his comrade and lunged at Munro. Collins had his pistol out by then. He couldn't risk the shot. He saw a blue arm shoot up and catch the Spokan's wrist. The chief came down on Munro. Breast to breast, they locked in struggle. The fierce, strained brown face and the war bonnet completely shrouded Munro's head.

Bullets made their cat-spit back and forth above the deadly struggle.

Beavers was wiggling desperately to roll aside the body of the Indian he had killed.

The soldier just ahead of Munro swung his rifle sideways. The butt knocked feathers from the war bonnet. The next blow struck the Indian's head, but still he hunched bare shoulders to free his knife hand. The soldier swung the rifle again. In a frenzy of short blows he pounded the Spokan's head.

The war bonnet slumped. Collins saw Munro's face. The lad had been biting at the Indian's ear and had a feather clenched in his teeth. The Spokan was out, and Munro still had his big left hand clenched hard on the wrist of the hand that held a knife.

"Shoot him now," Babcock said to the soldier who had beaten the chief unconscious.

No one had to shoot the Indian. Bullets whispering through the ferns struck the Spokan from both sides of the depression. Munro rolled him partly up the little slope, then looked wildly at his comrades.

"You did fine, Billy," Beavers said.

Some of the wild, scared look went from Munro's eyes. He felt at his side to find his rifle.

Collins pushed himself backwards. "Go up ahead of me, Babcock. Cut those ropes the next time they move the logs in front of those guns."

Lips and chin smeared with tobacco juice, Tobe Babcock crawled ahead. When he saw the logs and the poles extending back over the rocks he knew what Collins had been talking about.

He had to wait for what seemed a long time, wishing all the while he had his own gun instead of this long-barreled Springfield.

When the logs walked aside he cut the right-hand rope with one shot. Before he could reload the other log was back in place to hide the muzzle, but the trunk he had released was lying against the other log. It took him two shots to get the left-hand rope. For a moment, while he was reloading, he thought the left log was not going to fall. Pressure from the weight of the first one leaning against it slowly pushed it over.

The gunners cranked their pieces in a frenzy. Lead raked the dead and dying on the rocky spine.

Tobe Babcock put a careful shot right above the left-hand streaks of flame. The ball crashed into the feed slot and jammed it.

Someone in Major Friskey's party drove a ricochet from wall to wall in the narrow granite opening above the right Gatling. The misshapen lead smashed the face of the gunner. He wasn't the first who had been killed behind the two guns that day, but now the logs were gone. No one wanted to try the crank of the one sound piece while troopers in the trees were sending bullets through the gap.

The word went back. Some had guessed it already from wild, exultant yells of those far enough up the hill to know the guns were silenced.

Blue men surged over the ridge exposed to rifle fire alone. And that began to recede as the Indians sensed their magic many-shooting guns were dead.

The Utes on the left flank of the Gatlings pulled back first, but their comrades on the cliff above continued to hold up the flank of the blue line. In front of the guns the little island of Shawnees and Delawares stuck fast and fought. They fought hard and well. They must have taken the words of Face to the Storm in holy earnest when he had said: "We will go no farther toward the western sun. We will die here fighting."

Most of them were dead among the rocks when a rush finally took the hill. The guns were gone.

Above the bottom of the left H-leg the two Gatlings that had been holding up Hickaman's brigade ran out of ammunition. The Indians took them away.

Both flanking attacks began to move. The center heard and drove in harder against the front. Slowly the blue men pushed the Indians up and up. Never had veterans from plains warfare seen their old foes give ground so stubbornly, even when holding a great advantage in elevation. As they fell back the Indians took a heavy toll, utilizing their long experience in masterful retreats. This time they had no women or children to worry about. Except for the flank where the Delawares and Shawnees lay, all Indian casualties were carried away.

The blue men went up, but they did not rush eagerly to make close contact with the ever-compressing mass ahead.

By sunset the south hills were won. By taking and holding the ground the soldiers achieved a victory, though it cost them five times more dead than losing cost the foe. Possession of the good, blood-soaked earth —not statistics—constituted a victory.

Two decisions on the hills above the north mesa resulted in that action becoming a repetition of what was happening across the valley: Cannibal Bullard read the trend and retired his two Gatlings deftly; Colonel Accola made a bold guess about the Gatling in the trees ahead of him. He decided that it might have been disabled from the fire of his men below the mesa edge. He took half his force across the purple flat and met light resistance.

Iron Buffalo and Bad Jaw by then were riding high on the north hills to reach the conference far ahead of

Gross's line. The warriors they had left behind melted away.

Accola's men got the Gatling that the Cayuse had jammed with small stones. They got the Cayuse alive, too. He had stayed to fight when the rest fled. Perhaps it was because of the gleaming brass casings he loved so well.

They were the last things he looked at before two troopers bound his hands and prodded him down the hill.

Both flank attacks against the hills above the top and bottom of the right H-leg began to pinch the Indians. The center moved in hard. The defenders fell back no less bitterly than they had across the valley, but they fell back, taking almost all their dead and wounded with them.

Before Montell's *wagenburg* the cavalry capered, gave riding demonstrations and flung long-range insults. They had won one great victory and had been severely mauled in their attack against the flank of the wagons. They had enough for the time. But many of them stayed before the wagons, hoping that another idiot would send out a small force to be butchered.

Soon they began to dwindle away toward the trees, riding to aid their comrades in the retreat from the hills. Montell paced back and forth, not too far from his bags of stores, and dared the remnants to come in for another fight.

Iron Buffalo and Bad Jaw reached the Indians in front of Gross just as the council was breaking. The Otter had about two thousand willing to follow him in a charge against the upper end of the valley. Cuerno and Red Bull had dissuaded the rest.

"It is too late now," Iron Buffalo said. "We are losing

the hills. Those before the wagon fort are going away."

So Gross's line did not have to meet a charge that might have carried through, with great loss on both sides, but which would not have changed the outcome of the battle.

Sunset came. The army had won. Old Stub and others knew it was a Cadmean victory. Some of those who hadn't been on the plain with Larkins' regiment, or in the trees, or waiting to be ridden down while holding Gross's lines talked about the fight as a great victory.

Along with the Gatling that had been fouled with small rocks the army recovered the ruined Wiard, still on the Piegan's legs. He shouldn't have been alive yet, but he was. A trooper finished him with a carbine shot. Like a few others the soldiers found in the rocks, the Piegan wasn't worth taking alive.

Montell took a personal interest in the one sound prisoner the army had captured, the Cayuse. While a few men high in the thickets were still being killed, Montell had two troopers hold the Cayuse on the ground face down. Two other soldiers took a leg apiece and forced the Indian's shins over a small fire. Presumably the Cayuse had a great deal of information about the Indians' light artillery.

He was stubborn. All he said when reddening flesh began to raise on his shins was: "*Nesika papa klaxta mitlite kopa sah-a-le.*" He said it twice, and then he would not talk at all.

"What did he say?" Montell asked his half-breed Walla Walla interpreter.

"He said, 'Our father who art above.'" The half-breed's flat black eyes didn't quite mask his hatred of Montell.

"Where'd the damned savage ever learn that?" the general asked.

"It's Nez Percé. He probably learned it in Whitman's mission up in Oregon." The interpreter looked away from the fire. "He won't talk, General. He don't look smart enough to know much about the guns anyway."

"I'll be the judge of that!" Montell said. He spoke to the soldiers holding the Indian's legs. "More heat."

Riding disconsolately to escape the scenes around the surgeons' tents, Old Stub came to where the Cayuse lay.

His voice was a trembling whisper. "Release that man!"

"My orders, General," Montell said. "The damned savage won't give information willingly."

Old Stub's dark eyes glittered with hell's fire. His voice was still a hoarse whisper. "*He* is a savage, Montell?"

Escorted by a detail in charge of Lieutenant Collins, who told Old Stub blandly that his fingers were still numb, the Cayuse was taken to the lower plain and released with a message to Iron Buffalo from Old Stub: *The Army will come again.*

With black hatred behind his gray face, Montell resolved that when the army fought again he, not Old Stub, would be the leader.

Dusk came softly to the green valley.

Surgeons sawed and cut and sewed. They perspired in tents that still held the heat of day, saying many times to orderlies: "Don't bother with any more like that. Bring the ones who have a chance."

The surgeons were too busy, too weary to argue with Sergeant Mullins when they wanted to amputate his arm. He went away with his arm in a splint, knowing that the wound might begin to seethe and bubble and make men sick from the stench and in the end kill him. But Sergeant Mullins was used to taking chances.

He decided he would go see how his men were. He didn't go anywhere. Sergeant Mullins suddenly slumped on the trampled grass before the tent. Men carried him to where rows of wounded lay on blankets, some staring blankly at the evening sky, some moving in their agony and crying out strange sentences and parts of sentences.

Dan Beavers and Munro came by looking for Mullins. They found him pale and conscious, and fed him from a canteen full of lukewarm soup Beavers had produced from God knows where. Half-cooked pieces of beef kept choking the mouth of the canteen, but Mullins drank almost a cupful before he complained the liquid was too hot. He told Munro to get his uniform straightened. Then Mullins fell asleep.

Beavers and Munro waited decently until a man on the sergeant's right, a young infantryman with a bullet through one lung, no longer needed a blanket. They took it and covered Mullins carefully.

While they were walking away Munro asked suddenly, "What happened to that headquarters lieutenant?"

"Him and that scout came off the hill together," Beavers said. "They was arguing about whether Army Springfields are any good."

For the second time that day Babcock had come unhurt down the mesa hill. He'd caught a horse and ridden to the wagons. Now he was back at the base of the south hill, digging. He wanted to put Geore Phillips where he had fallen, but the ground on the purple flat was too close to granite. However, from where the grave lay you could see the upper end of the green valley and a long blue and white stretch of Shining Mountains

Phillips and Babcock had first seen as youths together thirty-nine years before.

The cold night came.

By torch and lanterns, details kept working to bring in wounded from among the rocks and trees. Surgeons seared their lips with bitter coffee from white cups held in bloody hands, then went back to work. They were out of medical supplies.

Men in outposts and picket lines along the hills and on the plains shivered in the cold and strained their eyes at shadows. Small groups of Apaches and Kiowas crept in with silent arrows and streaking knives, then went shrieking into the night. Statistically they did small harm. They kept the outposts wide awake. Before an alert, suspicious sentry shot him dead, a Cheyenne in a soldier's coat and forage cap went down a picket line and put arrows into three men.

The shouts and shooting kept the army restless.

Neither Old Stub's aides nor those they got to help them could find Corporal Thompson, the courier from Freeland. It was assumed that he lay dead somewhere. Much later it was assumed that he had been captured. Old Stub merely wanted to question him about Freeland. Though the general hoped for the best, reason made a cold and brutal weight inside him when he thought of Freeland's force.

No one found the courier.

Tobe Babcock didn't care that night how a corporal had smelled so long ago, the night before. Babcock was busy beside a large fire with tools he'd borrowed from a farrier sergeant. Babcock had torn a heavy granite rock from the south mesa hill and was chiseling the stone, laboriously copying letters someone had written for him. Phillips' name was misspelled, but Babcock didn't know that.

And Phillips didn't care.

So the few who had been concerned quit thinking about Corporal Thompson, the only courier who had ridden between the armies. He was cited, and many years afterward his mother received a Purple Heart and another medal from a grateful War Department that had been cleaning out old files. The corporal deserved the medals, though the citation was not accurate.

The real Corporal Thompson had fought like a demon to lead his little group to the top of Ute Canyon with Colonel Trevarthen. That his body had been stripped by a white man known among the Indians as Sunfish, then mutilated until unrecognizable by Gros Ventres, had been no fault of Corporal Thompson's.

He earned the medals, like hundreds who did not get them.

Night covered all. It masked greedy lights in the eyes of a young white man called Sunfish, now riding with Sarsi Indians nearing a high mountain pass, knowing that Bad Jaw would keep his word about sacks of gold.

Night took some of the rolling wildness from Cannibal Bullard's bulging eyes. He rode behind his guns, the guns he might have told Old Stub about—if more than one man in all the world had not been born with the name Accola.

Night covered two brothers who crawled from behind a dead horse that blocked the entrance to a shallow tunnel at the bottom of steeple-crowned cliffs. They had lived through rifle fire and attempts to burn them out with flaming brush. Their faces were strained and grimy, their hands and tunic sleeves were scorched. They listened to the silence of the night for several minutes.

Then they went down a little gulch to find the body of a bearded man who had saved them.

They couldn't find a body. An hour later they were fired upon by a nervous outpost, but they identified themselves and got inside the lines.

Old Stub's face showed nothing when the couriers made their report. The general could have been forgiven for cursing about a decision made three weeks too late. His face showed nothing.

Night enabled She Who Rides, Iron Buffalo and Bad Jaw to slip through the picket lines and look for old Fighting Bear. They found him in a crevice part way down the rock from which he had signaled. He was still holding his gilt-framed mirror in cold, stiff hands. The old Brule could have got away, but maybe he was tired from his long, futile ride to save a white brother that morning. She Who Rides spoke what was in her mind.

"He did not want to get away. He knew that there is only one end to war with the white men."

There in the dark of the blood-smeared hillside Iron Buffalo and Bad Jaw must have known the truth when they heard it. But by the time they had carried Fighting Bear's body outside the picket lines, they were already framing plans for the next battle.

The army rested badly. Men couldn't sleep, or else they moaned and muttered in their sleep. Three times Billy Munro woke yelling, clutching at a wrist, a wrist that in his dreams was too powerful to hold.

Men startled from their own restless sleep spoke angrily. "What in hell's the matter with him!"

Beavers shook the lad and waked him. "He's got a feather in his teeth."

"Stuff his whole mouth full of feathers!" someone said.

Before noon the next day five hundred of Freeland's men came in. They had fled down the valley and gone up the same canyon in which Masterson's command had been killed. With them were six of Masterson's rear guard who had escaped into the rocks below the flaming canyon.

Two days later, having buried its dead, the Army went slowly down the broad, peaceful, rolling grasslands on its return to Camp Pike. Behind it were burning supplies, destroyed to make room for wounded in the wagons. Ambulances were literally slopping full. More graves marked the going.

On a hill among the trembling trees Iron Buffalo watched. They would return, he knew. He had known before Fighting Bear said so, before the Cayuse brought the message from the little soldier chief.

Like a wolf that licks its wounded leg after being gored by a buffalo, the blue army would rest, then seek the Indians again. Wiser and more deadly, the soldiers would return.

Peace was now something that only the Big Bellies and the women would talk about.

Fighting was the only way, and the Indians were few. They were very few, Iron Buffalo thought, remembering the many villages he had seen all the way from the wide, muddy Father of Waters to the place called Washington.

But, unless the Indians wanted to die in places where there was no air to breathe, no land to ride across, no game to hunt and no far places to look up, they would have to fight—even as the Shawnees and Delawares had fought before the many-shooting guns. If freedom came from dying, then freedom was worth the price, Iron Buffalo thought.

With heavy heart the slender, poorly clad Indian limped to his pony and rode away.

Steve Frazee was born in Salida, Colorado, and for the decade 1926–1936 he worked in heavy construction and mining in his native state. He also managed to pay his way through Western State College in Gunnison, Colorado, from which in 1937 he graduated with a Bachelor's degree in journalism. The same year he also married. He began making major contributions to the Western pulp magazines with stories set in the American West as well as a number of North-Western tales published in *Adventure*. Few can match his Western novels, which are notable for their evocative, lyrical descriptions of the open range and the awesome power of natural forces and their effects of human efforts. *Cry Coyote* (1955) is memorable for its strong female protagonists who actually influence most of the major events and bring about the resolution of the central conflict in this story of wheat growers and expansionist cattlemen. *High Cage* (1957) concerns five miners and a woman snowbound at an isolated gold mine on top of Bulmer Peak in which the twin themes of the lust for gold and the struggle against the savagery of both the elements and human nature interplay with increasing, almost tormented intensity. *Bragg's Fancy Woman* (1966) concerns a free-spirited woman who is able to tame a family of thieves. *Rendezvous* (1958) ranks as one of the finest mountain man books together with such excellent works as Guthrie's *The Big Sky* and Gulick's *The Mountain Men*. Not surprisingly, many of Frazee's novels have become major motion pictures. According to Bill Pronzini in the second edition of *Twentieth Century Western Writers*, a Frazee story is possessed of 'flawless characterization, particularly when it involves the clash of human passions; believable dialogue; and the ability to create and sustain damp-palmed suspense.'

N 139 60
N 141·47
C 187·73

790·03 -